THE AMBITIOUS TEEN

DISCOVER YOUR PATH, PLAN YOUR CAREER,
AND NAVIGATE YOUR FUTURE LIKE A BOSS

MARNIE DAVID

CONTENTS

Disclaimer

Although the publisher and the author have made every effort to ensure that the information in this book was correct at press time and while this publication is designed to provide accurate information in regard to the subject matter covered, the publisher and the author assume no responsibility for errors, inaccuracies, omissions, or any other inconsistencies herein and hereby disclaim any liability to any party for any loss, damage, or disruption caused by errors or omissions, whether such errors or omissions result from negligence, accident, or any other cause.

The publisher and the author make no guarantees concerning the level of success you may experience by following the advice and strategies contained in this book, and you accept the risk that results will differ for each individual. The testimonials and examples provided in this book show exceptional results, which may not apply to the average reader, and are not intended to represent or guarantee that you will achieve the same or similar results.

INTRODUCTION

Picture this: it's a brilliant day in June. You can almost taste the sweet summer blossom scents in the air. The sky is clear, the grass is lush, and the birds sound excited... It's as if everything has converged for this moment.

The sun-drenched crowd buzzes with excitement as you spot your mom, who seems to be beaming like the summer sun.

Then your eyes meet your kid brother.

"You look so weird," he mouths...

You contemplate sticking out your tongue. But that would be childish. It's your high school graduation ceremony, after all.

As the principal *blah-blah-blahs* about wishing your entire class the best with your futures, your eyes wander.

That's when you notice something interesting.

Emily, one of your classmates, has enthusiasm and confidence written all over her face. She has known for years that she wants to be a marine biologist, and she's so ready to pursue her dream career.

But right next to you, Justin stares blankly ahead. Just last week, you heard him ranting about how he wished everyone would stop asking him what he wanted to do with his life. He's never really known what he wants to become, and he hates the idea of rushing a choice just because it's expected right now. Now that school is over, he is drowning in uncertainty about what's next.

Do you want to know something surprising, though?

Only around 50% of teens and young adults know what they want to do for a living. This means half of all your friends and classmates (and perhaps you, too) are looking at their futures without a clear direction of where they want to go. But even your classmates who *say* they know their dream careers can very easily change their minds in the future. In 2018, the Pew Research Center found that not even 30% of adults were in the careers they had set out to pursue when they were teens.

Not knowing your next move is kind of like being lost in the middle of the ocean with no land in sight.

It's pretty scary.

The pressure to choose a career path as early as possible can make the transition from your teen years to adulthood extra stressful and put a serious dent in your confidence.

Whether you're in your early teen years, about to finish high school, or somewhere in between, you should know that you are not alone in your struggles. Even if you have a good idea of what you want to do, crafting out a clear plan to get there can feel daunting. Or maybe you simply want to keep your options open. Exploring multiple avenues can help you learn more about yourself. Who knows…you might just discover new interests that lead you down an exciting new path!

In any case, this book can help you deal with:

The Overwhelm and Pressure to Choose a Career Path Early

"So, what do you want to do for a living?"

Urgh. How many times have you been asked that question?

It's as if the world expects you to have your entire life planned out before it begins. It can create an awful, queasy feeling, especially if you *really* don't know what you want to do when adulthood comes.

The Struggle of Identifying Your Interests and Strengths

Sure, high school exposes you to a ton of subjects and extracurriculars, but figuring out what makes you tick is way easier said than done.

The Feeling That You Don't Have Support and Guidance

By now you are either entering the stage of your life where you realize that your parents don't have *all* the answers, or you've known for a while. (Sorry, Mom and Dad, but it's true—I say this as a fellow parent). Even when your parents give advice, sometimes it feels like it is for someone else. The same goes for the school counselors and the mentors you may chat with. Not getting helpful answers can make that ocean you're trying to navigate feel even bigger than it actually is.

A note to parents, guardians, and mentors: a fresh perspective can make a huge difference in how your teen views and approaches career planning, and this book offers just that. It's not that your input doesn't matter. In fact, my hope is that you'll work through this book with your teen so you can help them navigate career planning with determination and an open mind.

Your Thoughts Around Financial Concerns and Constraints

The thought of student loans, job security, and whether your education will pay off can add a whole new layer of stress to your decision-making process.

Social And Peer Pressure

Ah, the weight of expectations. Your parents, friends, classmates, and even society at large can add a ton of pressure and easily leave you feeling like you *must* choose this or that career just to fit in.

Being confronted with constant questions about your after-school plans and hearing what your friends' and classmates' plans are at the same time is overwhelming.

- It can make you wonder if there's something wrong with you.
- It can make you feel like you're being forced into a decision.
- It can lead to choices you'll regret later.

So, whether you're craving clarity and a map like Justin, or brimming with passion but hoping for some guidance like Emily, you're at the crossroads of your future. Sooner or later, you'll have to give your next big move some serious thought.

But you already know that—it's why you're reading these words. No matter how you landed here, you know it's time. You're ready for guidance on career planning, because you're eager to discover more about yourself and what you're capable of doing in this world.

So, what's in it for you if you spend a little time each day reading this book?

You'll Gain Early Insight

This book will help you start thinking about your career path early, which will give you the time and freedom to make informed choices and avoid rushing into something that doesn't align with your strengths and interests.

What you'll learn in these pages can serve you well for the rest of your life, and allow you to wave goodbye to the overwhelming confusion and stress that often accompanies major life decisions.

In my home, we have a saying: *Sooner rather than later, but rather later than never.*

So, if you're around sixteen to nineteen, relax. In the greater scheme of things, you're still very young and you have enough time to figure things out. This book will not only make it easier, but it'll also make it a fun ride.

Self-Discovery

Through short quizzes and self-assessments, you'll get to know yourself better. Self-awareness is a crucial skill for making the right decisions for *you*, and the foundation you need to carve out a career that genuinely excites you.

Expert Guidance

You won't be going at it alone. We'll tap into the wisdom of teachers, school counselors, and professionals who have been in your shoes. It's like having a whole team of mentors in your corner cheering you on without fail.

You'll Explore a Wide Range Of Career Options

Together, we'll think about your future from inside and outside the box. We'll peek inside various career clusters, including STEM, business, creative fields, and more, allowing you to explore all kinds of possibilities—perhaps ones you haven't thought of yet.

You'll Get Your Hands Dirty (In A Good Way)

A big part of *The Ambitious Teen* is about implementation. It'll help you set realistic goals, write your resume, and develop networking skills to give you a running start into the world of work.

You'll Look into Alternative Paths

Not feeling the traditional college route?

No problem.

The book has you covered with info on vocational schools, certification programs, and the ambitious world of entrepreneurship. At the end of the day, this book is all about helping you craft out the path that suits *you* best.

***The Ambitious Teen* Is Your Personal Roadmap to Success**

Think of this book as your own personal career GPS, offering step-by-step guidance for achieving your career goals.

From the initial planning stages, all the way to landing your dream job or starting your own business, you can be sure that you'll have a supportive, guiding hand along the way to minimize all that confusion and worry.

Career planning should be fun.

With this book, it can be.

Take a minute to reflect on a future where the weight of uncertainty has been lifted, replaced by a sense of direction, purpose, and excitement about what lies ahead. **Wouldn't it be great to know you're on track to a fulfilling career that aligns perfectly with your passion and skills?**

Well, you can. *Now* is the time to take control of your future like a boss.

Ready to start crafting your success?

It starts by simply flipping the page. So, see you in Chapter One!

CHAPTER 1
THE STARTING LINE

 "The future depends on what you do today."

MAHATMA GANDHI

"Seriously? How am I supposed to choose a career when I don't even know what I'm most passionate about? Or what I want for dinner on most days?"

Chloe's dad blinked, unsure what to do next.

Her reaction was way out of character, because she had always been the calm one among his three daughters.

"Sorry, Daddy," she finally said and looked at her feet. "But there's like a million choices out there. I'm so confused."

———

Chloe isn't alone. Career choices have always been difficult to make, but I'll throw it straight at you—your generation has it *really* bad when it comes to all the options.

My generation (this includes your parents) was the last one born in an era where humans were still figuring out how to build and live in a world interconnected with tech.

Well, that world is here now, and you're the ones who will take it further.

They say a whopping 85% of jobs that will exist in 2030 haven't even been invented yet. (That's not even ten years from now!)

Crazy, right?

And here comes a huge paradox… It's both an exciting and scary time to be a teen for the exact same reason: endless possibilities.

But you know what?

Whether it's exciting or scary is ultimately in *your* hands.

Remember: you can never control the stuff that happens around you, but you can *always* control what you do about it.

Feeling overwhelmed is normal, and it's OK. But you want to avoid getting so caught up in those feelings that you become indecisive, because indecision is a real buzz killer. It stresses you out, makes you anxious, and makes you feel helpless.

Trust me, it's better to make a mistake by choosing "wrong" than not to choose at all. That's because when you make a mistake, you can at least learn from it and let experience guide you when you make the next choice. But when you don't choose, you stagnate.

Now, I'm not saying you're going to make a career choice that's *not* right for you. After all, this book is about giving you the tools you need to make the best choice that aligns with your strengths, values, and who you really are. All I'm saying is you shouldn't live your life avoiding making mistakes at all costs, and you should never allow the fear of making them hold you back from going out there and living your life.

This chapter is not about making choices just yet. You've got plenty of time for that, even if it feels like your friends, parents, teachers, coaches, and anyone who's someone expects you to decide *now*.

Breathe.

You've got this.

For now, we're just going to chat about why it's important to start thinking about what comes after school. This is an opportunity for self-discovery, and it comes with the added benefit of giving your future self a little head start toward success.

THE IMPORTANCE OF EARLY CAREER PLANNING

"Come over here," Chloe's dad said as he sat down at the kitchen table.

"Can we do this later?"

"Sure," her dad said in an amused tone, "how about when you're thirty?"

Chloe smiled as her dad chuckled and patted the open chair next to him.

"It'll only take a couple of minutes, kiddo."

Chloe joined her dad, still feeling overwhelmed by the idea that she'd have to make a big decision in the near future. Her dad placed a comforting hand on her shoulder.

"These feelings are okay. We're a team in this, okay? Your mom and I are here to support you, and there are people who can help you work through this."

Chloe's smile didn't quite reach her eyes. "But why is career planning such a big deal, Dad? Can't I just go with the flow and figure things out along the way?"

"Mm…" *Her dad nodded as if in deep thought.* "Well, you could, but think of it this way: imagine you're going on a road trip. You could just drive off into the unknown and hope you'll stumble upon something interesting. But what if you miss out on breathtaking places and experiences because you didn't plan ahead?"

Chloe pondered her dad's analogy. "So, career planning is like plotting my route on the map of life?"

"Yup. It can give you purpose. You can set goals and make informed decisions. It's just a fact of life that when we have plans, we're more likely to make the most of life's opportunities. And it can really help you discover your passions along the way."

"Huh…" *Chloe's shoulders straightened.* "I guess career planning is a tool to take control of my future. Like, it can help me make choices based on what I want and prevent me from just drifting without direction."

"Exactly," *her dad said and put his hand on her shoulder again.* "But, remember, you don't have to lock yourself into a specific career choice right now. That's not what this is about. Just make an effort to explore your interests, discover your strengths and weaknesses, and gradually pave a clear path for your future."

Chloe nodded as the stress about career planning started lifting.

"Your career is no different than life in general, kiddo. It's made up of a series of steps, and each one brings you closer to your goals."

———

The chat with Chloe's dad helped her gain the perspective she needed to look at career planning and self-discovery as something positive, and it gave her a sense of determination to start thinking about what she'd like to do with her life after high school.

But what if she somehow lost this newfound determination and decided that, after all, she'd figure things out later?

Surely, there's no harm in choosing this path, right?

Let's find out.

THE PRICE OF DELAYING CAREER PLANNING

It leads to missed opportunities

Rarely does anyone stumble upon amazing opportunities by mere luck. The truth is, opportunities come to those who actively pursue them. By postponing career planning, you risk missing out on experiences that could set you on an exciting and fulfilling path.

Keep in mind: you may have time on your side now, but it shoots by faster you expect. And opportunities, like time, wait for no one.

It causes higher stress levels and increased anxiety

As graduation creeps closer, external pressure intensifies. This can lead to significant stress and anxiety, making it even more difficult to make crucial life-changing decisions. Without a career plan, you might end up feeling rushed to choose and end up in a career you hate.

Limited flexibility

Many teens misunderstand career planning, fearing it will lock them into a fixed path. In truth, it's about charting your course while preserving flexibility. Delaying this process can limit your adaptability and limit your ability to pivot if your initial choice doesn't fit. Starting early offers room to explore without stress.

Money, money, money… there's a high price on procrastination

Decisions you make now are going to impact your financial future. Procrastination is like snoozing an alarm—it gives immediate satisfaction but it messes up your entire day. In this case, your entire future is at stake. While you're sitting on the fence, your peers might be building savings from earning in their dream jobs. Not to mention how you might struggle to make ends meet or deal with old student loans that don't even fit your career path. Early planning aligns your education and career goals, ensuring smart financial decisions and a rewarding payoff in the long run.

You might look back with regrets and what-ifs

Regrets are part of life, but minimizing them by living fully is crucial. Career planning is different from impromptu adventures, for which you'll have plenty of time. Postponing planning increases the chances that you'll one day look back and come up with endless "what if" scenarios. Once the regret sets in, it can linger for years, affecting your happiness and well-being.

THE REWARDS OF EARLY CAREER PLANNING

Phew... that was gloomy! But those risks and downsides are totally avoidable, and you have the power to determine how things are going to play out in your future. Let's see what could happen if Chloe stayed determined to focus more on career planning.

Knowledge: clarity in a fast-paced world

Feeling lost in the crowd of endless career options? Well, in a rapidly changing world, early career planning brings clarity. It ensures you can navigate the chaos and select a profession that suits your personality, strengths, and goals.

Self-awareness: finding your perfect fit

Career planning builds self-awareness.

Understanding your skills, competencies, and interests helps you make confident choices in the sea of career options.

Self-development: building essential skills

Early planning nurtures essential qualities like discipline, focus, and determination, traits that will serve you well in the long run. Adaptability to life's changes will be crucial as you grow and your goals evolve.

Confidence: unshakable self-belief

If you've read *The Confident Teen*, you'll know confidence comes from many places and is influenced by many factors. You can gain immense confidence from charting your path, knowing where you're heading, and being in control.

Increased creativity and motivation

Having a clear career plan ignites your creativity and fuels your motivation. When you know what you're working toward, you're inspired to think outside the box, explore new ideas, and find innovative solutions. Your passion for your chosen path propels you to excel and keep those creative juices flowing.

Visibility: getting noticed and recognized

Alignment with your career plan (that is, your interests, passions, and strengths) ensures job satisfaction and excelling in your chosen field. People take notice when you love what you do, which sets the stage for growth and promotion.

Retirement plan: securing your future

Yeah... It sucks to think about retirement when you haven't even officially entered adulthood, but career planning isn't just about right now or the next few years. It prepares you for a comfortable future, ensuring you can look back with satisfaction and enjoy the rewards of your hard work.

Peace of mind: less stress, more focus

Career planning replaces uncertainty and stress with purpose and focus. This peace of mind extends to all aspects of life and promotes your overall well-being.

To career plan or not to career plan... that's the big question!

Because this whole career planning thing was still new to Chloe, she sometimes had doubts about whether it would REALLY have a big impact on her life. So, one day, she sat down to weigh planning vs not planning against each other. When she was done, she KNEW career planning was the way to go. Here's what helped her make that decision:

Early Career Planning	Late or No Career Planning
✓ Proactively create your own opportunities	✗ Miss out on opportunities
✓ Enjoy confidence decision-making	✗ Experience intense pressure and anxiety
✓ Flexible career choices with the ability to pivot if necessary	✗ Lock yourself into a rigid path
✓ Smart financial planning	✗ Potential to struggle financially
✓ Less regrets and more fulfillment	✗ Lingering regrets and what-ifs
✓ Clear career path	✗ Lack of clarity and direction
✓ Laser focus on your strengths and interests	✗ Lack of self-awareness
✓ Strong foundation for success	✗ Slow self-development
✓ High confidence	✗ Low confidence
✓ Endless inspiration	✗ Lack of creativity and motivation
✓ High chance of getting recognition for your achievements	✗ Mediocracy and limited visibility
✓ Look forward to a comfortable retirement	✗ Totally unprepared for retirement
✓ Focus and well-being	✗ Stress and uncertainty

Self-assessment quiz: What's my career awareness level?

Career awareness is all about having a good sense of what you enjoy doing and what you're good at. It's about understanding the different jobs and careers out there and how they might match up with your interests and skills. When you're career-aware, you know what kind of work might make you happy and how to plan for it in the future.

The below quiz will help you gauge your current level of career awareness. When you're done, we'll chat about how to interpret the results and what you can do about it.

Section 1: Self-Reflection

For each question, choose the answer that best describes your feelings and experiences. Rate your responses on a scale from 1 to 5, with 1 being "Strongly Disagree" and 5 being "Strongly Agree."

*Each number represents points (e.g., "3" is 3 points).

1. *I have a clear understanding of my interests and passions.*

- 1
- 2
- 3
- 4
- 5

2. *I know my strengths and what sets me apart from others.*

- 1
- 2
- 3
- 4
- 5

3. *I feel confident about my ability to achieve my career goals.*

- 1
- 2
- 3
- 4
- 5

Section 1 score: _____

Section 2: Career Knowledge

Rate your knowledge level for the following statements (choose the option that best represents your thoughts and feelings).

1. I am aware of various career options available in my areas of interest.

- In the dark (1 point)
- Some knowledge (2 points)
- Good understanding (3 points)

2. I know the educational or training requirements for my desired career.

- Limited knowledge (1 point)
- Basic understanding (2 points)
- Well-informed (3 points)

Section 2 score: _____

Section 3: Career Planning

Answer the following questions about your career planning efforts.

1. Have you ever created a career plan or set career goals for yourself?

- Never (1 point)
- I've thought about it (2 points)
- Yes, I have a plan (3 points)

2. Do you actively seek out information or opportunities related to your career goals?

- Rarely (1 point)
- Occasionally (2 points)
- Frequently (3 points)

Section 3 score: _____

MY TOTAL SCORE: _____

How to interpret your assessment results:

If your score is...

1–7: You're in the early stages of career awareness. Don't worry; everyone starts somewhere! Focus on exploring your interests and identifying your strengths. Consider taking career assessments or talking to a career counselor to gain more clarity. More on this in Chapter 3.

8–14: You have some career awareness, but there's room for growth. Start by researching different career options within your areas of interest and setting clear career goals. Consider reaching out to professionals in your desired field to gain insights.

15–21: You have a good level of career awareness. Now, let's take your planning to the next level. Create a detailed career plan with short-term and long-term goals. Actively seek opportunities and experiences that align with your chosen path.

Create a game plan based on your results:

Early career awareness (score 1–7)

- Identify your strengths and skills through self-reflection and feedback from others.

- Do career interest assessments to explore your passions and interests.

- Join clubs and extracurriculars you think you might enjoy. (You can always leave if you find out it's not for you, but you'll never know if you don't take action.)

- Ask your closest family members, friends, and mentors what they believe your interests are. (Sometimes, outsiders are more perceptive of what makes us tick than we are. But don't just take their word for it. Make a list of people's suggestions and then explore whether it's true for you. You'll know if something resonates with you or not.)

- Once you have a better picture of what interests you, begin researching different career options within those areas.

Developing career awareness (score 8–14)

- Create a simple career plan that outlines your short and long-term goals. This is a lot like writing down a to-do list for your future. Short-term goals could be things you want to accomplish in the next year, like getting good grades, joining a club, or volunteering. Long-term goals are bigger, like picking a college or a career.

- Connect with professionals in your desired field to gain valuable advice and insider perspectives. If you build a relationship with someone in your dream field, they might let you shadow them some time (you'll spend a day or two with them at the office or in the field to see how they do their work).

- Start seeking out internships, part-time jobs, or volunteer opportunities related to your chosen career. Immersing yourself in the industry can help you see if it really is what you want to do.

Established career awareness (score 15–21)

- Develop a detailed career plan. This entails clearly defining your ultimate career goal (as in, "I want to be an entrepreneur in field XYZ") and setting up milestones and action steps for yourself to stay on track.

- Actively seek opportunities, join professional organizations, and attend relevant events to network with professionals in your desired field.

- Continuously assess your progress to make sure you're reaching your milestones toward achieving your ultimate goal.

- Practice a lot of self-awareness so you can be mindful of any significant changes in your interests.

- Adjust your career plan as needed.

Knowing your career awareness level is empowering and helpful, because it gives you the mental space to visualize your next steps. But it is equally important not to get hung up on your career awareness level. It doesn't matter if you're at the early or established stage. All that matters is what you decide to do with it.

———

TLDR: WHY BOTHER WITH CAREER PLANNING NOW?

Too long, didn't read? Check out this section at the end of every chapter for a recap of what we've learned.

In Chapter 1, I've shown you how planning your career now can be the key to a happier, more successful you. Here's why it really matters:

- **Overall Well-Being:** Early planning gives you clarity, confidence, and peace of mind, positively impacting all areas of your life.

- **Avoid the Pitfalls:** Procrastination can lead to missed opportunities, financial difficulties, and regrets.

- **Unlock Your Potential:** Proactive career planning empowers you to develop skills, gain control over your future, and ultimately achieve a fulfilling career path.

Now that you know the risks of delaying your career planning and the benefits of engaging in it early, it's time to start crafting your future.

Ready? See you in Chapter 2.

CHAPTER 2
UNDERSTANDING YOUR CAREER CONTEXT

 "May your choices reflect your hopes, not your fears."

NELSON MANDELA

areer aspirations don't form in a vacuum. For every human, major life choices are influenced by our families, schools, friends, and the expectations in our cultures and societies. It's important to recognize this so you can be mindful of the big "why" behind your decisions, because while we can't escape these influences, we shouldn't allow them to dictate our lives, either.

At the end of the day, you're still *you*. You have your own mind, your own voice, and your own life to live. You totally have a say (the biggest say, actually) in the shaping of your future.

In this chapter, we'll reflect on the external influences that play a role in your choices and talk about how to navigate their impact on your career planning.

THE INFLUENCE OF EXTERNAL FACTORS

Family

Perhaps your parents are immigrants and you feel an obligation to make them proud by taking on a career they'll approve of. Maybe there's an unwritten rule that you're supposed to take over the family business one day. Or, perhaps, you come from a long line of doctors and you're pretty convinced your parents have assumed that's what you'll pursue, too. If you have an older brother or sister who has already started their career, they can also affect how you perceive your own future. And, of course, you might have a favorite aunt or uncle you look up to for inspiration.

Whatever the case, there's no question that family dynamics play a big role when you start thinking about a career path.

Let's look at Sam's life as an example.

His dad was an easy-going guy and he wanted his kids to be happy, but he also wanted them to make the most of their potential. He believed in them. So, although he never tried to push them into specific careers, there had always been that expectation that they'd choose something, well… "respectable".

Sam's oldest sister was a real estate agent. One of his brothers was an acclaimed marketing professional at a big corporation. And his other brother graduated at the top of his class as a lawyer.

Here's the deal: familial influence can be both a source of support and pressure.

For Sam, it leaned more toward pressure.

He was the odd one out. His aspirations included writing and traveling the world, and he wanted to take the unconventional route—something like becoming a content creator so that he could support his dream lifestyle.

But something told him this idea wouldn't sit well with his dad, especially because he always talked about how Sam might enjoy journalism or perhaps a career in marketing, like his one brother.

———

Whether you feel support or pressure from your family, their thoughts, feelings, and expectations mean a lot to you, which is why they have so much influence over your decision-making process.

School

All those hours you spend at school can have a significant impact on your career interests. Maybe there's a teacher who sparked your curiosity about science or literature, or perhaps an elective course led you to discover a hidden talent. School can open doors to new possibilities and steer you towards certain fields you might not have considered otherwise.

Society

You may not even be aware of it, but your broader community has a say in your thought processes, too. Societal norms and expectations are very real, which means they naturally influence your career choices and the options you're willing to consider.

The Hunger Games is an extreme case, but it does a great job illustrating the above phenomenon. If you were born in District 12 with Katniss, you'd choose coal mining or something related to the industry, and if you were born in District 4, you'd take up something related to fishing. Likewise, in the real world, your neighborhood, community, city, and whatever you get exposed to while interacting with them can guide you in specific directions.

SELF-REFLECTION: WHAT INFLUENCES ME THE MOST?

Take a moment to think about the various factors at play that are shaping your career aspirations. Recognizing these influences will help you make informed decisions about your future.

Family ties

Consider the role your family plays in your career choices. Have their values, expectations, or experiences influenced your aspirations?

- Yes
- No
- I'm not sure…

If I'm unsure, why do I feel that way? (Skip this question if you chose 'yes' or 'no')

_____

_____

_____

_____

_____

_____

Do I see my family's influence on my aspirations as a good or bad thing, and why? (If you chose 'no', reflect on how it could be a good or bad thing.)

_____

_____

_____

_____

_____

_____

_____

What do you think your parents or guardians expect you to choose as a career? Think about whether this is something you're just assuming or whether you know it for a fact. Write your thoughts in the appropriate spaces below.

I **assume** my parents/guardians want me to...

_____

_____

_____

_____

_____

_____

Because...

_____

_____

_____

_____

_____

_____

_____

OR

I **know for a fact** my parents/guardians want me to…

_____

_____

_____

_____

_____

_____

Because…

_____

_____

_____

_____

_____

_____

.   .   .

When I really think about it, do I resonate with what my family expects me to choose? Why or why not?

_____

_____

_____

_____

_____

_____

_____

School impact

Reflect on your school experience. Have specific teachers, courses, or extracurricular activities inspired you to pursue a particular field? And how have these experiences shaped your interests and goals?

_____

_____

_____

_____

_____

_____

_____

Societal pressures

How has your community or society at large influenced what you're considering as a career?

_____

_____

_____

_____

_____

_____

_____

Are there societal norms or expectations that you feel pressured to conform to even though you don't fully agree? What are they?

_____

_____

_____

_____

_____

_____

_____

What values or trends in your society influence your thinking? This is a deep one, so take your time to really reflect and be honest with yourself before jotting your thoughts.

_____

_____

_____

_____

_____

_____

_____

This is ME...

If your family's and society's expectations didn't exist, if there was absolutely no pressure from anyone or anything, what would you choose as a career?

Important note: this is a serious question, so don't say "sit around and watch movies all day" or anything unrealistic. Be honest about the ONE thing you'd love to do for the rest of your life if it all depended on you. If you don't know what that is yet, write, "I'm not sure" and add the date. Remember: There's zero shame in not knowing what your ideal career is—this book is here to help you figure it out.

_____

_____

_____

_____

_____

_____

_____

BALANCING INFLUENCE AND AGENCY

No matter from which angle you try to approach it, there will always be an interplay between external influences and what _you_ really want to do.

This is true for all major life choices. Your career is just the starting point, and career planning is the perfect playing ground to learn the importance of staying true to yourself while recognizing and being empathetic of those external influences, because those influences aren't "things" ... Eight to nine times out of ten, they're people you either look up to or care about.

In 2021, Joblist shared some statistics[1] that proves just how much influence family and society have on individuals' career choices.

For instance, a staggering 48% of adults who took part in the study believed that their parents had a strong influence on their career choices. Around 40% admitted that they felt pressured to follow their parents' advice about their career paths, and more than half said they felt like their parents had forced them to go to college.

But... And this is a big but, so pay attention:

Two out of every three parents who participated in the study felt disappointed that their kids never chose *their* desired career paths.

Here's a bit of wisdom you can carry with you and share with your grandkids one day: humans tend to overcomplicate life by not communicating with each other and by making way too many assumptions.

Your mom and dad might feel compelled to give you advice simply because they're more experienced than you in this thing called life, **but they want you to be happy, no matter what**.

Yes, I admit that some parents absolutely don't want to hear that their children have other plans than what they envision for them, but this scenario happens less often. If you happen to be the kid of strong-willed parents, I hope they're reading this book

---

1. https://www.joblist.com/trends/the-impact-of-parental-influence-career-edition

so they can remember how they felt when they were your age. Either way, as you dive deeper into the book, you'll learn valuable ways to navigate and balance their influence with what you want. But the most important tool is this:

Finding balance between your family's expectations and your desired path starts and ends with clear communication

Clear communication is the art of expressing your thoughts, feelings, and ideas in a way other people can understand. It also has an empathetic aspect, which means even though you've got your opinion, you're open to the other person's opinion and you're willing to consider their point of view. Here's how to do it:

Don't assume, ask

You know how sometimes you think you know what your parents or guardians want for you?

Well, don't be so sure.

Instead of guessing, just ask them. Ask about their hopes and dreams for you, and when the opportunity arises, let them know about yours. You might be surprised by what you learn. Like, your parents might be more open to your dreams than you think. Asking questions can help you understand each other better and bring you closer together.

But knowing what to ask can be tough to figure out, I know. Here are some ideas to get those conversations started:

1. What did you dream of becoming when you were my age?
2. Are there any careers you think would be a great fit for me?
3. Do you have any concerns or worries about the career I want to pursue?

4. How do you see me achieving my dreams? What steps do you think I should take?
5. Can you tell me more about your own career journey and the lessons you've learned?
6. What values or principles do you think are essential for me to succeed in any career?
7. Is there anything specific you'd like to see me achieve in my future?
8. What do you think are the pros and cons of the career I'm interested in?
9. Can you share any stories from your own life where you had to make tough career decisions?
10. If I didn't choose a career you think is a good fit for me, would you still love and cheer me on?

Remember, the more you talk with your parents or guardians, the easier it will become to find a balance between their expectations and your dreams.

Watch your tone and be nice, even if you feel your mom or dad doesn't "get" you.

When you're talking about your future, emotions can run high. It's okay to feel strongly about your dreams, but it's also important to show respect for your parents' feelings and ideas.

Remember the saying, "You catch more flies with honey than with vinegar."

That means speaking kindly and politely is more likely to get you what you want. If you get emotional, don't worry or be too hard on yourself, it's all part of growing up and learning how to talk about the important stuff. Here are some practical tips for keeping a cool head:

- **Take deep breaths:** If you feel yourself getting worked up or angry during the conversation, take a few deep breaths. It can help you stay calm and collected.

- **Use "I" statements:** Instead of saying, "You just don't understand me," try saying, "I feel strongly about this career path because…" This way, you're expressing your feelings without blaming your parents.

- **Stay open-minded:** Even if you disagree with your parents, try to listen to their perspective. You don't have to agree, but showing that you're willing to hear them out can go a long way.

- **Avoid accusations:** Instead of saying, "You're not supportive of my dreams," try saying, "I'd love to have your support as I pursue my passion." It's less confrontational and more likely to yield a positive response.

- **Know when to step away:** If the conversation is getting too heated or you feel like it's turning into a fight, it's okay to say, "I need some time to think about what we've discussed. Let's continue this later." This allows both you and your parents to cool off and regroup when you're calmer.

- **Listen and be open to your parents' ideas:** Communication is not just about you talking; it's about listening, too. When your parents share their thoughts and concerns, really take in what they're saying. They have life experience and wisdom, and listening to them is a way of showing respect. Sometimes, they might have insights you haven't thought about. Besides, being open to their ideas helps them feel valued and can lead to better discussions. If they say something that you don't fully understand or would like to know more about, ask them questions.

- **Keep these conversations flowing:** Just because you've had the career talk with your parents once, it doesn't mean everything is settled now. Whenever there's an opportunity, reinforce your interests and passions and plans. And if there's a shift, like maybe you discover something that really makes you curious enough to reconsider your intended path, talk about it with your parents. Ask them for advice on how to deal with this new interest. They'll appreciate your honesty and might even give you some guidance. Open communication builds trust. By keeping the conversation flowing, you ensure your parents stay involved.

Bottom line: communication is the key to finding the right balance between what your family wants for you and what you want for yourself. And remember: it's your career, but involving your family in it can make it even more exciting and worthwhile.

DEALING WITH SOCIETY'S INFLUENCES ON YOUR ASPIRATIONS

Societal expectations are kind of sneaky, because they have a subtle way of wriggling themselves into the subconscious mind. You don't realize their influence before you start thinking about life-changing decisions like your career, where to buy a house, what car to drive, where to send your kids to school…

Societal influences can be good for you or they can push you into a box you absolutely don't belong in. When you're young, it's hard to resist these influences (whether good or bad), because you have an innate need to belong and prove yourself.

But the older you get, the more you'll realize you have the power to attract your own tribe—people who share your values, beliefs, ideals, and even your opinions—by simply being yourself.

You *already* belong, and your people will find you.

Whatever you end up doing for a living, consider this piece of advice: your choices should always reflect your aspirations and passions, not just what society expects.

There's no fool-proof way to resist societal expectations. Even adults struggle with this, but you'll care less as you mature. In the meantime, use the following tips to your advantage:

- **Build your support network:** Surround yourself with friends and mentors who encourage your dreams and respect your choices–much more on this in the next chapter.

- **Know why you want to head in that specific direction:** People are weird… We have a tendency to undervalue or dismiss things we don't understand. So, when talking about your aspirations and career path, use it as an opportunity to educate and inspire people about that job or industry. If you're confident and passionate, the person you're talking with will listen and respect your choices, even if they don't understand them.

- **Find inspiration from society's outliers:** Seek out those individuals who have defied societal expectations by relentlessly pursuing their dreams. The best news? These people aren't rare—there are countless success stories of people going against the grain and achieving remarkable results.

- **Love what you do:** Money alone won't make your world go round. Yes, financial stability is important, but so is enthusiasm and dedication, because those are the factors that will ensure a fulfilled life. So, don't be tempted by what society says will be a great career choice for a teen in your position. Focus on finding your passion and stick with it. The money will follow.

- **Ignore the stereotypes:** If you're a guy interested in nursing or a girl interested in computer science, go for it. Embrace your interests without hesitation. The idea that men and women belong in specific careers is ancient, so never be afraid to challenge it by pursuing whatever you want.

- **Engage in as much self-discovery as possible:** Take the time to understand what truly excites you and where your talents lie. By knowing yourself well, you can make choices that align with your genuine desires.

Your career is going to become a significant part of your identity, so it's super important that your choice reflects your values and interests. Don't let societal expectations limit your potential— ever. You live in a free country, so embrace that freedom and make choices that empower you to live a life of passion and purpose.

———

Despite Sam's concerns about disappointing his dad, he insisted that he wanted to take a gap year before going to college. He took that time to travel and, being away from the influences at home, he took the opportunity to start vlogging about the places and attractions he visited.

His gap year turned into a three-year traveling adventure most people can only dream of. These days, he has his own tribe and he's earning enough money to support himself from his content business.

But here's the kicker: Sam is now studying part-time to get his journalism degree. During his travels, he discovered impoverished communities in desperate need of humanitarian help. This made him realize that he doesn't want to write about just anything—he wants to share these people's stories with the world and play an active role in raising funds to uplift their communities. His dad couldn't be prouder.

———

See? Personal agency doesn't necessarily mean dismissing external influences. Often, there's an opportunity of harmonizing those influences with your aspirations. But if you don't stand up for yourself and what you want, you might miss your true purpose.

Sam might never have discovered his purpose if he hadn't insisted on taking that gap year. It's also true that he probably wouldn't have discovered the vehicle to drive that purpose (journalism) if it wasn't for his dad's influence. That's why it's never a bad idea to listen to the opinions and advice of your family members regarding your future. However, if you don't agree with their ideas, you have a responsibility toward yourself and them to clearly communicate your side of the story.

TLDR: NAVIGATING THE MAZE OF INFLUENCES

Your career choices are influenced by your family, school, and societal expectations, but they shouldn't define your path. Instead of letting these influences dictate your future, you can take control of your career journey by:

- **Embracing Self-Discovery:** Take the time to understand your interests, strengths, and values so you can reflect on what you really want.

- **Challenging Stereotypes:** Don't let societal expectations dictate your dreams.

- **Cultivating Support:** Surround yourself with people who believe in you and your aspirations.

- **Communicating Openly:** Talk to your family about your career goals and find a balance that respects both your dreams and their expectations.

- **Following Your Passion:** Ultimately, make choices that empower you to live a life of passion and purpose.

You are unique, so align your career choices with *your* values and interests. By doing so, you'll build a life filled with enthusiasm and purpose. After all, your career isn't just a job; it's a chance to express your passions and make a meaningful impact.

I hope you feel more empowered to make choices that resonate with who you are and your purpose. But who's in your corner when doubts arise? Who can guide you when you feel lost? In the pages that follow, we'll uncover how to build a supportive team to cheer you on every step of the way.

See you in Chapter 3.

CHAPTER 3
YOUR SUPPORT NETWORK

“ "Surround yourself with the dreamers and the doers, the believers and thinkers, but most of all, surround yourself with those who see greatness within you, even when you don't see it yourself."

SERENA WILLIAMS

E ver watch Serena Williams dominate the tennis court at Wimbledon and wonder how she achieved such legendary status? Those 23 Grand Slam titles didn't come from nowhere. And it wasn't just pure talent that got her there either. Nope, Serena had a whole squad backing her up, from her parents, who introduced her to tennis and supported her every step of the way, to her coaches, who fine-tuned her skills and pushed her to be the best. This support system was a huge part of her success.

The same goes for you and your career. You don't have to do it all alone. Building a crew of people who believe in you, challenge you, and cheer you on can be a total game-changer. Let's dive into how you can build this dream team to help you reach your full potential.

TEAM MEMBER #1: YOUR GUIDANCE COUNSELOR

Guidance counselors are often an untapped resource. While their role in scheduling classes and resolving school conflicts is well-known, their expertise in career and college planning often goes unnoticed. These unsung heroes can be a huge part of your support network, offering valuable advice and guidance as you figure out your next steps.

The great thing about guidance counselors is that they're trained to help you explore diverse career paths, uncover scholarship opportunities, and plan your future. They are brimming with experience and knowledge, and they're eager to share it with you.

Why Counselors Are Your Secret Weapon

Let's take a look at how Mayra's school counselor, Ms. Rodriguez, made all the difference in her journey:

Mayra felt like she was walking on eggshells at home. Every conversation seemed to end in frustration, with nobody truly understanding her. Needing a safe space to vent and a neutral perspective on her future, Mayra decided to take a chance and pop into Ms. Rodriguez's office during her lunch break.

Taking a deep breath, Mayra hesitantly opened the door. Ms. Rodriguez's warm smile immediately put her at ease. "Come in, Mayra," she said, gesturing to a chair. "Is everything alright?"

Relief washed over Mayra as she explained her situation. "I feel so lost, Ms. Rodriguez," she confessed. "College applications are looming, and I have no idea what I want to do with my life. I think Science is really interesting, but lately, I've been feeling this huge pull toward art."

Ms. Rodriguez listened attentively, nodding as Mayra poured out her heart. Instead of offering a quick fix, Ms. Rodriguez offered something far more valuable - understanding.

"Mayra," she said with a gentle voice, "it's completely normal to feel torn between different paths in life. The good news is, your future isn't limited to one box. You can absolutely find a way to combine your passions– there are no rules saying you have to choose just one."

Mayra's eyes widened. This perspective, one she hadn't considered, shifted the weight on her shoulders. A flicker of hope ignited within her.

"Thank you, Ms. Rodriguez," she said, her voice filled with genuine appreciation. "I've been so stressed about making the wrong decision, but you've really helped me see things differently. Maybe there's a way to have both science and art in my life."

Ms. Rodriguez smiled kindly. "That's the attitude, Mayra! Just remember, it's okay to explore different paths and take your time figuring out what's best for you. There's no rush. And if you ever need someone to talk to again, my door is always open."

Leaving Ms. Rodriguez's office, Mayra felt a huge weight lift off her shoulders. While one conversation didn't magically solve everything, it did make her feel heard and supported. The future seemed less daunting, and Mayra wondered why she hadn't popped into the office sooner.

Did you see how Ms. Rodriguez offered a listening ear and a fresh perspective, without pushing her own opinion? That's the beauty of having a counselor – they're your personal cheerleaders, dedicated to helping you succeed, and bound by confidentiality to keep your conversation private.

Bottom line: Reach out to your school counselor, whether it's for guidance, support, or even just to vent. You'll leave feeling lighter and more confident about your future–I promise. It's a simple step that could be the catalyst for your future success.

Steps to Take Before Your Meeting:

1. Get Clear on Your Why: Before you schedule your meeting, take a few minutes to think about what you are hoping to get out of this conversation. Are you looking to explore specific career paths, brainstorm college options, or simply get some guidance on your next steps? The clearer you are about your goals, the more productive your meeting will be. Here are some things to think about before your meeting:

- What am I passionate about?
- What are my strengths and weaknesses?
- What kind of environment do I thrive in?
- What kind of impact do I want to make in the world?
- What do I want to achieve in my career?

By thinking about these topics beforehand, you'll be able to steer your conversation in the right direction. Your counselor will get a clearer picture of what you're hoping to achieve, and you'll walk away with advice that's actually helpful and relevant to you.

2. Take Your Career Assessments: Your counselor may suggest taking some assessments beforehand to help you gain a deeper understanding of your personality, interests, and potential career paths. Two common assessments you might encounter are:

- **Myers-Briggs Type Indicator (MBTI):** This test identifies your personality type based on how you see the world and make choices. Knowing your MBTI type can be pretty eye-opening, helping you understand your strengths and weaknesses, and even pointing you towards careers that might be a good fit.

- **Holland Code (RIASEC):** This assessment is like a career matchmaker. It looks at what you're interested in and what you're good at, then suggests career paths that might be a perfect match for you. It's a great way to explore different options and see what sparks your curiosity.

While these assessments aren't the be-all and end-all of your career choices, they can be extremely insightful. They can help you understand yourself better, figure out what you're really good at, and even point you toward careers that might be a good fit.

3. Send an Email: To make your meetings as productive as possible, take charge. Email your counselor beforehand with specific topics you'd like to discuss. This proactive approach ensures you get the most out of your sessions. Plus, you'll go into the meeting feeling less nervous.

To get those wheels turning, here are some great questions you can ask:

About Your Personality and Career Tests:

- What do you identify as my strengths?
- Which careers do you think match my strengths?
- Where do I need to improve?
- How can I work on improving these areas?

About Your Grades:

- What kind of grades are colleges looking for?
- Which AP or honors classes should I be taking?
- Can we look over my transcripts together?

About College:

- Do you have any college brochures about the careers I'm interested in?

- Can you connect me with some current students at the colleges I'm thinking about?
- What are the pros and cons of attending a college away from home?

About Careers:

- Are there any upcoming career fairs in the area?
- Are there any career speakers scheduled to visit our school?
- Can you connect me with people currently working in my chosen career?

It's possible that your counselor might offer advice that you don't entirely agree with, and that's okay. They base their opinions on their observations of you and the results of their assessments. While you aren't obligated to follow their advice, it can be valuable when combined with your own research. Keep in mind that their perspective should be one of many that you consider, just as a single assessment should not be the sole factor in your career decisions.

4. Come Prepared

When meeting your counselor, bring any important documents or materials. This could be a college essay, report cards, test scores, letters of recommendation, or anything else related to your school or activities. Having these things ready helps your counselor understand you better and offer personalized advice. Plus, it shows them you're serious about planning your future. So, go in prepared, ask all the questions you want, and let your counselor be your guide.

TEAM MEMBER #2: TEACHERS

Did you know that the adults who spend the most time with you in an academic setting are your teachers? They're not just there to grade your tests; they're also your mentors, your advocates, and your biggest fans in the academic world. They've witnessed your growth, your struggles, and your triumphs in the classroom, giving them unique insights into your strengths and potential – insights that can be incredibly valuable as you explore your career options. Not convinced? Let's dive into why teachers are the perfect people to have on your career support team.

They Know You Better Than You Think

Think about a time your teacher noticed something special about you, whether it was your knack for creative writing, your talent for problem-solving, or your ability to lead a group project. Teachers see you in action every day and often pick up on your hidden talents and untapped potential. This valuable insight can help you identify your strengths and explore career options you might not have considered.

They're Honest

Teachers can offer constructive criticism to address areas where you can improve. Maybe you need to work on your study habits or develop better skills like communication and teamwork. Don't take this as negativity; embrace it as an opportunity for growth. Their honest feedback can help you address your weaknesses and maximize your potential, paving the way to greater success in your future.

So, teachers have a pretty good read on your strengths and weaknesses. But how can you turn that knowledge into career gold? By tapping into their expertise and perspectives, teachers can help you develop the skills they already see in you, ultimately guiding you towards a fulfilling career path. Here's how:

Exploring Career Options

Since your teachers have a front-row seat to your strengths and interests in action, they can witness firsthand what subjects you excel in and what activities you naturally gravitate towards. This unique perspective allows them to offer personalized guidance as you discover what you really want for your future self.

For example, if your teacher sees you shine in debate class, they might suggest exploring law or politics. If you're a natural at coding, they could point you towards exciting tech careers. And if you're always the first to volunteer for group projects, they might encourage you to consider management or leadership roles.

Beyond simply suggesting career paths, teachers can help you reveal hidden talents, connect your existing skills to specific industries, and even introduce you to professionals already working in fields that interest you. This guidance can be invaluable as you clarify your goals and develop a clearer vision for your future career.

Academic Planning

Similarly to guidance counselors, teachers are experts in academic planning. They can help you choose the right classes, understand academic requirements for different majors and colleges, and suggest extracurricular activities that will enhance your college applications. Their expertise can help you create a strategic plan to achieve your academic and career goals.

Resources Galore

Your teachers are a treasure trove of resources for your career journey. They can recommend books, articles, and websites that can expand your knowledge about different careers and industries. They can also connect you with alumni who have pursued similar paths and organizations that offer internships or mentorship programs. Their connections and knowledge can open doors to opportunities you might not have discovered on your own.

The takeaway: teachers are invested in your success, both inside and outside the classroom. They want to see you thrive and achieve your full potential. Don't hesitate to tap into their expertise and guidance as you navigate your career exploration journey.

Building Meaningful Relationships with Your Teachers

The relationship between students and their teachers is often built on trust, respect, and mutual understanding. The first step to seeking support from your teachers is to build meaningful relationships with them. Here's some tips to get you started.

- **Initiate Conversation:** Don't be afraid to chat with your teachers about what interests you, your goals, or any worries you might have. You can pop by during office hours, catch them after class, or shoot them an email. However you choose to connect with them, know that talking openly can help you build a stronger connection and get some really useful advice.

- **Seek Feedback:** Take the plunge and ask your teachers how you're doing in class. They're usually more than happy to give you tips on how to improve. You could send a simple email like this:

Hey Mr. Geller,

. . .

Hope you're doing well! I was wondering if you could give me some feedback on how I've been doing in class lately. I really value your advice, and I think your input could help me get even better.

Thanks,

Mayra

- **Follow Up:** After getting advice or feedback from your teacher, make sure to take action and then follow up with them. By reaching out to them, you're showing that you're serious about getting better and that you value their input.

Ultimately, your teachers know you well and can provide insights into your strengths and weaknesses. Also, they're an excellent resource to support you as you figure out your career path. The key is to keep the lines of communication open, ask for feedback when you need it, and follow up with your teachers often.

TEAM MEMBER #3: EXTENDED FAMILY

Jake, a high school sophomore with a growing interest in computer science, decided to reach out to his older cousin, Owen.

Owen was a successful software engineer at Google, and he was someone Jake admired. Fueled by excitement and a desire for guidance, Jake sent Owen a text, suggesting they grab coffee and chat about their shared love of technology and coding.

Owen was thrilled to hear from his younger cousin, and enthusiastically agreed to meet. They planned to catch up at a cozy local café known for its excellent coffee, a perfect environment for a meaningful conversation.

During their meet-up, Jake bombarded Owen with questions. He wanted to know everything about Owen's career path, the realities of being a software engineer, and the skills needed to thrive in the computer science field.

Owen wasn't afraid to tell it like it is. He weaved in stories from his own career, showing Jake the good, the bad, and even the sleep-deprived nights fueled by pizza and coffee.

As their conversation flowed, Owen shared more and more practical advice. He offered tips on building coding skills, how to network with the right people in the field, and even what classes to take in college. He also explained how Jake could ace those internship interviews and how to stay on top of the ever-changing world of software development.

Leaving the café, Jake felt empowered and inspired by Owen's guidance and support. He had not only gained valuable knowledge but also found a trusted mentor and ally in his cousin.

In the days and weeks that followed, Jake and Owen remained in touch. Jake reached out for advice, shared updates on his coding projects, and sought feedback on his programming skills. Owen continued to offer encouragement, support, and valuable advice as the newest member of Jake's support network.

How to Reach Out to Family Members

Let's unpack how Jake brought his cousin Owen into his support squad. Jake began by thinking about his extended family and considered which family members had careers he thought were interesting. Then he remembered Owen, who had an impressive job at Google.

Who in your family can you connect with? Maybe you have an Aunt who's been a teacher for 20 years. Or it could be an uncle who runs his own pizza restaurant. Perhaps it's a second cousin who has her own YouTube channel. Think about your cousins, aunts, uncles, or retired grandparents—they can all be valuable sources of support and guidance as you navigate your career. While these family members may not be as closely involved in your daily life as your immediate family, they can open up new perspectives and experiences in your life. Plus, you never know if they have connections that can get you that dream job.

Where to Connect

Take advantage of family gatherings, reunions, or virtual meetups to connect with relatives who work in fields that align with your interests or have valuable wisdom to share. Use these opportunities to engage in meaningful conversations about your career aspirations and seek their advice on navigating the job market. Your extended family may be able to offer helpful guidance, share industry-specific knowledge, or provide networking opportunities that can help you advance in your chosen field.

If meeting up in person is not in the cards, you can also connect with extended family members through social media, email, or phone calls. Share updates about your academic and career achievements, and express your interest in learning from their experiences and insights. Building and maintaining relationships with these family members can open doors to new opportunities and expand your support squad as you navigate your career path.

Don't forget to thank your family for their support. Their experiences are a goldmine of wisdom. When you actively engage with your family, you'll strengthen your support squad and glean practical advice that will bring you so much closer to success.

WHY A SUPPORT SQUAD IS IMPORTANT

Building a strong support network of family, counselors, and teachers can be an invaluable tool in career planning. Here's why it matters:

- **Emotional Support:** Career decisions can be a rollercoaster ride of emotions. It's easy to feel overwhelmed, stressed, and unsure of yourself. That's where your support network comes in. Your family, counselors, and mentors create a safe space for you to express your doubts, anxieties, and frustrations without judgment. They offer a listening ear, a shoulder to lean on, and words of encouragement to lift you up when you need it most.

- **Practical Advice:** Family, counselors, and mentors can be your sounding board as you brainstorm ideas, your guide through tricky decisions, and your warning system for potential roadblocks. They've been there, done that, and made their own share of mistakes along the way. Their real-world experience is like a cheat sheet for success, so don't hesitate to tap into their wisdom.

- **Opportunities:** A strong support squad isn't just about advice and encouragement; it's also about opening doors to a world of opportunities that you might not discover on your own. Your network can connect you with valuable resources, introduce you to influential people in your field, and even help you land that coveted internship or job.

Seeking help and guidance from others is a smart move, not a weakness. Your support squad—teachers, mentors, family, and friends—can offer a wealth of wisdom, experience, and resources that you can tap into to propel yourself forward. Lean on their expertise, bounce ideas off them, and let their encouragement fuel your ambitions.

TLDR: BUILDING YOUR CAREER SUPPORT SQUAD

A strong support network is essential for navigating your career. To recap, here's how to assemble your team:

- **Lean on Your Guidance Counselor:** They're trained experts in career and college planning, ready to offer personalized advice and support. Don't hesitate to schedule a meeting and ask questions.

- **Tap into Your Teachers' Expertise:** Your teachers know your strengths and weaknesses. They can offer valuable insights, connect you with resources, and provide guidance as you explore different career paths.

- **Engage Your Extended Family:** Reach out to family members who have careers that interest you. Their real-world experience and connections can provide valuable advice and open doors to new opportunities.

With a solid understanding of yourself and a supportive crew by your side, you're ready to embark on the exciting journey of career exploration.

Looking ahead, I'll guide you through a step-by-step approach to pinpoint the ideal career path for you.

See you on the other side.

CHAPTER 4
FINDING YOUR IDEAL CAREER

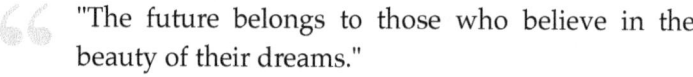

"The future belongs to those who believe in the beauty of their dreams."

ELEANOR ROOSEVELT

Imagine wandering into a bookstore, eager to discover your next favorite read. But instead of neatly organized sections, you're faced with a chaotic jumble of books. Fiction and non-fiction intermingle, biographies bump up against cookbooks, and self-help guides share shelf space with thrillers. You're surrounded by endless possibilities, but the lack of order makes it impossible to navigate. Each shelf might hold a hidden gem, but the overwhelming chaos makes it nearly impossible to find what truly speaks to you.

Now, envision your career trajectory as a journey through that very same bookstore. The world is brimming with diverse career paths, each with its own unique twists and turns. Without a map or guide, you could easily find yourself wandering aimlessly, unsure where to begin.

This is where *career clusters* come in. Just like bookstore sections categorize books by genre, career clusters group similar jobs together based on shared characteristics, allowing you to pinpoint specific areas that align with your interests and strengths.

Consider this chapter your personal librarian, helping you navigate the shelves of the career bookstore and discover the perfect "read" that aligns with your passions and aspirations.

WHAT ARE CAREER CLUSTERS?

Career clusters divide thousands of jobs into 16 groups based on shared skills, knowledge, and industries–providing you with an organized map of the professional world.

Here's an overview of the 16 career clusters with some example jobs:

———

#	Career Cluster	Example Job
1	Agriculture, Food & Natural Resources	• Farmer Agricultural Engineer • Forester • Environmental Scientist • Animal Scientist
2	Architecture & Construction	• Architect • Civil Engineer • Construction Manager • Electrician • Landscape Architect
3	Arts, Audio/Video Technology & Communications	• Graphic Designer • Film Director • Public Relations Specialist • Audio Engineer • Animator
4	Business Management & Administration	• Accountant • Human Resources Manager • Marketing Specialist • Business Analyst • Operations Manager
5	Education & Training	• Teacher • School Counselor • Education Administrator • Instructional Coordinator • Paraprofessional
6	Finance	• Financial Analyst • Bank Teller • Investment Banker • Financial Planner • Auditor

7	Government & Public Administration	• Politician • Public Administrator • Government Analyst • Urban Planner • Diplomat
8	Health Science	• Nurse • Doctor • Medical Laboratory Technician • Physical Therapist • Pharmacist
9	Hospitality & Tourism	• Hotel Manager • Chef • Travel Agent • Event Planner • Tour Guide
10	Human Services	• Social Worker • Counselor • Rehabilitation Specialist • Child Care Worker • Family Therapist
11	Information Technology	• Software Developer • IT Manager • Data Analyst • Cybersecurity Specialist • Network Administrator
12	Law, Public Safety, Corrections & Security	• Lawyer • Police Officer • Correctional Officer • Firefighter • Paralegal

13	Manufacturing	• Production Manager • Quality Control Inspector • Machinist • Welder • Industrial Engineer
14	Marketing, Sales & Service	• Sales Representative • Advertising Manager • Customer Service Representative • Market Research Analyst • Retail Manager
15	Science, Technology, Engineering & Mathematics (STEM)	• Engineer • Scientist • Mathematician • Biochemist • Statistician
16	Transportation, Distribution & Logistics	• Truck Driver • Logistics Coordinator • Air Traffic Controller • Supply Chain Manager • Warehouse Manager

Take a moment to look through this chart and think about the people in your life—neighbors, parents, relatives—and try to match their jobs to the career clusters listed. It's amazing how thousands of jobs can be organized into just 16 categories, right? Now, reflect on your own thoughts and feelings about these clusters and jobs. Put a star next to any that pique your interest, a question mark next to those you're curious about, and an X next to the ones that just don't resonate with you. This is your first step towards discovering what kind of career might be a good fit for you, so have fun with it.

Finding Your Ideal Career Cluster

To find a career cluster that fits you like a glove, it's important to get to know your unique interests and skills. Think of it like this: your interests are the things that make your heart beat a little faster, the activities that you lose yourself in and genuinely enjoy. Your skills, on the other hand, are your strengths—the things you're naturally good at or have honed through practice and experience.

Interests: Your Passion Fuel

Your interests are the subjects, activities, or areas that spark your curiosity and enthusiasm. When you're genuinely interested in something, time seems to melt away—you're completely absorbed, in that sweet spot often called "flow." And when you're doing work you truly enjoy, earning a paycheck feels like a bonus because it doesn't even feel like work.

Skills: Your Superpowers

Your skills are your unique set of abilities, honed through education, training, and life experiences. These can be technical skills, like coding or design, or soft skills, like communication, leadership, or problem-solving. Remember those times your teachers recognized your talents? Those are clues to your superpowers – the skills that make you stand out. These are the abilities that will help you thrive in your chosen career, enabling you to tackle challenges, collaborate effectively with others, and make a real impact in your field.

THE SIX INTERESTS AND SKILLS CATEGORIES

Let's take your interests and skills and categorize them further. You can group them into six broad categories, often called the Holland Code in career counseling (Remember that career test your guidance counselor might give you? This is it!). The six categories the test looks at are:

1. **Realistic (Doers)**
2. **Investigative (Thinkers)**
3. **Artistic (Creators)**
4. **Social (Helpers)**
5. **Enterprising (Persuaders)**

6. **Conventional (Organizers)**

Each category aligns with specific *career clusters*, helping you find jobs that match your profiles. Let's break down these categories and see which career clusters pair up with them.

Category #1: Realistic (Doers)

Realistic doers are all about action. They thrive on hands-on work, using tools and their practical skills to create tangible results. You'll find them in construction, agriculture, manufacturing, and other fields where they can build, repair, or operate machinery. They're the problem-solvers who get things done, always focused on the task at hand.

If you are a realistic doer, you probably have the following interests:

- Working with hands
- Mechanical tasks
- Outdoor activities

And you also probably have the following skills:

- Technical proficiency
- Physical coordination
- Tool operation

Here are the Career Clusters that align with Realistic Doers:

Category #1 Realistic (Doers)	
Career Cluster	**Example Job**
Agriculture, Food & Natural Resources	• Farmer • Agricultural Engineer • Forester
Architecture & Construction	• Architect • Civil Engineer • Construction Manager
Manufacturing	• Production Manager • Quality Control Inspector • Machinist
Transportation, Distribution & Logistics	• Truck Driver • Logistics Coordinator • Air Traffic Controller

Category #2: Investigative (Thinkers)

Investigative thinkers are the curious minds of the world. They love digging into complex problems, analyzing information, and figuring things out. You'll find them in science, research, and other fields where they can use their brains to uncover the truth. They're not afraid to ask questions and challenge the status quo. They're always seeking knowledge and understanding, driven by a desire to make sense of the world around them.

If you are an investigative thinker, you probably have the following interests:

- Research
- Solving puzzles
- Science and math

And you also probably have the following skills:

- Analytical thinking
- Research abilities
- Problem-solving

Here are the Career Clusters that align with Investigative Thinkers:

Category #2: Investigative (Thinkers)	
Career Cluster	**Example Job**
Health Science	• Nurse • Doctor • Medical Laboratory Technician
Science, Technology, Engineering & Mathematics (STEM)	• Engineer • Scientist • Mathematician
Manufacturing	• Production Manager • Quality Control Inspector • Machinist
Information Technology (IT)	• Software Developer • IT Manager • Data Analyst

Category #3: Artistic (Creators)

Artistic creators are the dreamers and visionaries who bring color and life to the world. They thrive on breaking the mold, pushing boundaries, and expressing themselves through their art. You'll often find them immersed in projects that allow them to unleash their creativity and create something beautiful, whether it's a painting, a sculpture, a piece of music, or a performance. They're the free spirits who add a touch of magic to the workplace, inspiring others with their unique perspectives and innovative ideas.

If you are an Artistic Creator, you probably have the following interests:

- Creating art
- Writing
- Performing

And you also probably have the following skills:

- Creativity
- Artistic talent
- Innovation

Here are the Career Clusters that align with Artistic Creators:

Category #3: Artistic Creators	
Career Cluster	Example Job
Arts, Audio/Video Technology & Communications	• Graphic Designer • Film Director • Public Relations Specialist
Writing and Publishing	• Author • Editor • Copywriter
Performing Arts	• Actor • Dancer • Musician
Visual Arts	• Illustrator • Art Director • Photographer

Category #4: Social (Helpers)

Social helpers are the empathetic souls who find joy in connecting with and assisting others. They thrive in environments where they can build relationships, offer support, and foster a sense of belonging. You'll often find them in roles like teaching, counseling, nursing, and social work, where they can directly impact people's lives. They're the caring and compassionate individuals who create a positive and supportive atmosphere wherever they go.

If you are a social helper, you probably have the following interests:

- Helping others
- Teaching
- Counseling

And you also probably have the following skills:

- Communication
- Empathy
- Teamwork

Here are the Career Clusters that align with Social Helpers:

Category #4: Social Helpers	
Career Cluster	Example Job
Education & Training	• Teacher • School Counselor • Education Administrator
Health Science	• Nurse • Doctor • Medical Laboratory Technician
Human Services	• Social Worker • Counselor • Rehabilitation Specialist
Hospitality & Tourism	• Hotel Manager • Chef • Travel Agent
Law, Public Safety, Corrections & Security	• Lawyer • Police Officer • Correctional Officer

Category #5: Enterprising (Persuaders)

Enterprising Persuaders are ambitious self-starters who thrive on taking charge and aren't afraid to take risks. They possess unwavering confidence and have a knack for persuading and motivating others. You'll often find them leading teams to achieve ambitious goals, closing deals, or inspiring others to reach for the stars.

If you are an Enterprising Persuader, you probably have the following interests:

• Leading
• Selling
• Debating

And you also probably have the following *skills*:

- Leadership
- Persuasion
- Strategic planning

Here are the Career Clusters that align with Enterprising Persuaders:

Category #5: Enterprising Persuaders	
Career Cluster	Example Job
Business Management & Administration	• Accountant • Human Resources Manager • Marketing Specialist
Marketing, Sales & Service	• Sales Representative • Advertising Manager • Customer Service Representative
Government & Public Administration	• Politician • Public Administrator • Government Analyst

Category # 6: Conventional (Organizers)

Conventional Organizers are the ultimate behind-the-scenes heroes. They thrive on order, structure, and accuracy, and they're the masters of details. You'll find them in fields like accounting, finance, and administration, where they excel at managing data, organizing information, and ensuring that everything runs like clockwork. They're the reliable, detail-oriented individuals who provide essential support and structure to any team or organization.

Interests:

- Organizing data
- Managing details
- Following procedures

Skills:

- Organizational skills
- Attention to detail
- Data management

Here are the Career Clusters that align with Conventional Organizers:

Category #6: Conventional Organizers	
Career Cluster	Example Job
Finance	• Financial Analyst • Bank Teller • Investment Banker
Business Management & Administration	• Accountant • Human Resources Manager • Marketing Specialist
Information Technology	• Software Developer • IT Manager • Data Analyst

The Holland Code Assessment

If you haven't taken the Holland Code assessment yet, you can easily find free versions of it online. This assessment will help you understand your interests and how they align with different careers. Here are two places where you can take the assessment online:

1. Truity's Holland Code Career Test

https://www.truity.com/test/holland-code-career-test

2. Career One Stop Interest Assessment https://www.careeron estop.org/Toolkit/Careers/interest-assessment.aspx

After you take the assessment, take another look at the career cluster charts. Ask yourself: which of these clusters spark your interest? Which ones seem like a good fit for your skills and personality? Let your curiosity guide you as you explore these options further and gain a deeper understanding of the diverse career paths available to you.

CAREER PATHWAYS

Now that you have a solid grasp of your interests, it's time to explore the specific paths you can take within your chosen career field. The good news? You don't have to wait until you have a college degree to get started in a field you're passionate about. Career pathways can guide you from your first job to a successful career, showcasing how you can develop your skills and education along the way. Let's dive into some real-life examples.

Cluster: Health Services Pathway: Therapeutic Services			
Level 1	**Education**	**What They Do**	**Moving Up**
Certified Nursing Assistant (CNA)	Short-term training program (and usually passing a state exam.)	Provide basic care to patients, help with daily activities, take vital signs, report patient concerns to nurses.	Licensed Practical Nurse (LPN) or Registered Nurse (RN).
Level 2	**Education**	**What They Do**	**Moving Up**
Licensed Practical Nurse (LPN)	One-year program from a technical school or community college.	Provide basic nursing care, give medications, monitor patient health, and assist RNs and doctors.	Become a Registered Nurse (RN).
Level 3	**Education**	**What They Do**	**Moving Up**
RN (Registered Nurse)	Associate's Degree in Nursing (ADN) or Bachelor of Science in Nursing (BSN).	Administer medications, coordinate patient care, perform diagnostic tests, and educate patients about health conditions.	RNs can specialize in areas like critical care or pediatrics, or pursue advanced roles like Nurse Practitioner (NP) with a Master's degree.
Level 4	**Education**	**What They Do**	**Moving Up**
Nurse Practitioner (NP)	Master of Science in Nursing (MSN) or Doctor of Nursing Practice (DNP).	Provide primary and specialty care, prescribe medications, and diagnose and treat illnesses.	NPs can further specialize, take on leadership roles, or contribute to healthcare policy and education.

Cluster: Information Technology Pathway: Software Development			
Level 1	**Education**	**What They Do**	**Moving Up**
Junior Software Developer	Associate's Degree in Computer Science or a coding bootcamp.	Write and test code, debug software, and help develop applications.	Gain experience and more certifications to move into more senior roles.
Level 2	**Education**	**What They Do**	**Moving Up**
Software Developer	Bachelor's Degree in Computer Science or a related field.	Design, develop, and maintain software applications, work with other developers, and meet with clients to discuss needs.	Developers can specialize in specific programming languages or types of software, like mobile apps or cybersecurity.
Level 3	**Education**	**What They Do**	**Moving Up**
Senior Software Developer	Bachelor's or Master's Degree in Computer Science, plus lots of experience.	Lead software projects, mentor junior developers, design complex systems, and ensure code quality about health conditions.	Senior developers can move into roles like software architect or IT project manager.
Level 4	**Education**	**What They Do**	**Moving Up**
Software Architect	Master's Degree in Computer Science or extensive professional experience.	Design high-level software architecture, set technical standards, and oversee the overall technical direction of projects.	Software architects can progress to chief technology officer (CTO) or other executive positions within tech companies.

Cluster: Finance Pathway: Financial and Investment Planning			
Level 1	Education	What They Do	Moving Up
Financial Analyst	Bachelor's Degree in Finance, Economics, or a related field.	Analyze financial data, create reports, and provide recommendations for investments and financial planning.	Analysts can get certifications like Chartered Financial Analyst (CFA) to enhance their credentials and move into senior roles.
Level 2	Education	What They Do	Moving Up
Financial Planner	Bachelor's Degree in Finance or a related field, plus certification.	Help clients develop financial plans, advise on investments, retirement, and estate planning.	Experienced planners can open their own financial planning firms or move into wealth management roles.
Level 3	Education	What They Do	Moving Up
Wealth Manager	Bachelor's or Master's Degree in Finance or Business Administration.	Manage the financial portfolios of high-net-worth individuals, provide investment advice, and develop wealth preservation strategies.	Wealth managers can become partners in wealth management firms or take on executive roles in financial institutions.
Level 4	Education	What They Do	Moving Up
Partner at a Wealth Management Firm	Bachelor's or Master's degree in Finance or Business Administration.	Owns a share of the firm, manages high-value client relationships, and helps set the strategic direction of the company.	Less common, but some partners may move into industry leadership roles with national financial institutions or consulting firms.

It's a lot less daunting to start your dream job when you understand how to climb the ladder from entry-level positions all the way to top-level roles. By taking small steps and having a plan for where you're heading, building a career becomes much more manageable. Let's explore how these career pathways can unfold in real life.

CASE STUDIES

Hearing real-life stories about how people just like you discovered their passions and built successful careers can be incredibly inspiring and helpful. The following stories showcase how interests and skills can guide your career choices, regardless of your background or level of education.

Case Study #1: Maria's Journey From CNA to Nurse Practitioner

Maria's career began as a Certified Nursing Assistant (CNA) right out of high school. She thrived on caring for patients and found deep satisfaction in the healthcare field. Driven by her passion for medicine, she continued her education while working part-time, eventually earning her nursing degree. As a Registered Nurse (RN), Maria specialized in pediatrics and furthered her studies to become a Nurse Practitioner (NP). Today, she combines her love for helping others with her medical expertise, working in a pediatric clinic where she makes a meaningful difference in the lives of children and their families.

Case Study #2: Cameron: Coding His Way to Success

Cameron discovered his passion for programming in high school, teaching himself various coding languages. He honed his skills through freelance projects, gaining valuable experience and building a portfolio of work. Eventually, he decided to pursue a degree in computer science, further solidifying his knowledge and opening doors to new opportunities. Today, Cameron is a software engineer at a leading tech company, developing innovative software solutions that impact millions of users worldwide.

Case Study #3: Corrie: The Marketing Maven Turned Entrepreneur

Corrie's journey began with a series of marketing roles after college. Throughout her career, she gained valuable experience in the industry, from social media marketing to brand strategy. Her passion for helping businesses thrive, combined with her entrepreneurial drive, eventually led her to take the leap and start her own marketing agency. Now, Corrie owns a company that specializes in helping small businesses develop and execute effective marketing strategies, leveraging her years of experience and knowledge to deliver great results.

Case Study #4: Noah's Creative Journey: From High School Doodles to Design Pro

Noah's artistic journey began in the hallways of high school, where he spent countless hours sketching and doodling, a passion that eventually blossomed into a full-fledged career. His love for digital art and graphics ignited a desire to pursue a degree in graphic design, where he honed his skills and developed a unique artistic vision. Today, Noah works for a renowned advertising agency, bringing brands to life through his visually stunning designs. He's living proof that turning your passion into a career is not only possible but incredibly rewarding.

Case Study #5: Camila's Green Dream: From Nature Lover to Environmental Engineer

Camila's passion for the environment ignited a spark in her to pursue a fulfilling career. Growing up with a deep love for nature and a growing concern for environmental issues, she knew she wanted to make a difference. This drive led her to pursue a degree in environmental engineering, where she could combine her scientific knowledge with her desire to protect the planet.

Today, Camila works on projects that tackle real-world environmental challenges, such as designing sustainable infrastructure, developing renewable energy solutions, and restoring damaged ecosystems. Her career allows her to not only utilize her engineering skills but also to make a tangible impact on the world around her.

These stories prove that you don't need to wait for a college degree to work your way up to your dream job. Career pathways show how you can develop your skills and education over time, ultimately finding fulfilling work. If you're passionate about a field, there's no reason to delay – get started now!

TLDR: FINDING YOUR PERFECT CAREER MATCH

Here's a quick rundown of how to discover a career that's just right for you:

Step 1. Explore the 16 Career Clusters: Start by familiarizing yourself with the 16 career clusters and the types of jobs they encompass. Think of it as browsing the different sections of a bookstore to discover your interests.

Step 2. Uncover Your Interests and Skills: Reflect on what excites you and what you're good at. Consider your passions, hobbies, and natural talents, and categorize them into the six Holland Code categories: Realistic, Investigative, Artistic, Social, Enterprising, and Conventional.

Step 3. Match and Research Career Pathways: Use your understanding of your interests and skills to choose a career path that sparks your passion and plays to your strengths. Then, dive deeper into the career options within your chosen clusters and pathways. Remember, it's okay to change your mind or explore different options as you grow and evolve.

Great job narrowing down those career clusters! Now, let's get you even closer to your dream job by exploring the different paths to get there. We'll cover everything from hands-on learning with vocational programs and apprenticeships to the college route and beyond. Knowing what kind of education you'll need, whether it's a certificate or a degree, will help you plan your next steps and find the perfect educational path that gets you where you want to go.

CHAPTER 5
EDUCATION OPTIONS

 "Your time is limited, don't waste it living someone else's life."

STEVE JOBS

D oes it feel like everyone around you is constantly chanting, "Go to college, get a degree, secure a good job?" Has there always been a part of you that's questioned this narrative? There have to be other options out there, right? Well, that's exactly what we're about to explore in this chapter because, let's face it, there's a whole universe of education possibilities, and college is just one of many paths to success.

WHY COLLEGE? THE TRADITIONAL VIEW

You've probably heard it a million times: college is the key to a bright future. It's often seen as the ultimate ticket to success, unlocking doors to fancy job opportunities, fat paychecks, and the chance to live the dream.

And guess what? There's some truth to that. Studies do show that people with a bachelor's degree tend to earn more money over their lifetime than those without one. Plus, having that diploma can open doors to all sorts of career paths that might otherwise be out of reach. So yes, college can definitely give your bank account a boost and set you up for some pretty fantastic job opportunities.

However, I'm here to tell you that college is not the only path. While college can be a wonderful option for many, it's definitely not the perfect fit for everyone. Some people thrive in hands-on environments, while others excel by starting their own business right out of high school. So, before you dive headfirst into the college admissions frenzy, take a moment to consider your options.

Types of Careers Requiring a College Degree

Let's dive into the kinds of jobs that pretty much demand a college degree. Think about fields like science, technology, engineering, and mathematics (STEM)—basically, the ones that need a lot of brainpower and specialized knowledge. Then there's healthcare, education, law, and business. These areas typically require you to have at least a bachelor's degree to get your foot in the door.

Field	Example Job Titles
Science	Lab Researcher, Wildlife Biologist, Lab Chemist
Technology	App Developer, Data Analyst, IT Support Specialist
Engineering	Building Designer, Software Developer, Electrical Technician
Mathematics	Risk Analyst, Data Scientist, Math Tutor
Healthcare	Registered Nurse, Physician, Pharmacist
Education	Teacher, School Counselor, Education Coordinator
Law	Lawyer, Paralegal, Legal Assistant
Business	Accountant, Marketing Manager, Human Resources Specialist

Take a close look at this list and circle any job titles that stand out to you. While a college degree is usually needed for these jobs, there are always exceptions, and you can still find other ways to succeed in these fields. But having that degree can really enhance your opportunities of landing a great position and boosting your income in these industries.

Pros and Cons

So, is college worth it? Well, that depends on who you ask and what their goals are. For some, it's the ticket to success they've been waiting for. For others, it might not be the right fit. Before you start filling out those college applications, let's take a moment to weigh the pros and cons.

Pros

- **Benefit #1: Higher Income Potential:** Studies have shown that college graduates earn an average of 84% more over their lifetime compared to those with only a high school diploma. This translates to about $1 million more in earnings over a 40-year career. With a degree, you're not just opening doors to more job opportunities;

you're also increasing your potential for a higher salary and greater financial security.

- **Benefit #2: Expanding Your Horizons:** College opens up a world of possibilities, giving you access to a wide range of industries and professions that might not be as easily available without a degree. In fact, a 2023 study found that 75% of college graduates felt their degree opened doors to new career paths and opportunities for advancement. But college isn't just about career options; it also equips you with the skills employers want, like critical thinking, problem-solving, and communication. Plus, it's a fantastic place to network and build professional relationships that can be super helpful throughout your career.

- **Benefit #3: Find Yourself:** College is more than just textbooks and exams; it's a transformative experience that shapes who you are and who you want to become. It's an adventure of self-discovery where you unearth hidden talents, passions, and values that guide you throughout your life. You might find your lifelong best friend in a dorm mate from across the country or discover a passion for environmental activism through a volunteer group you joined on campus. Living on campus opens doors to a vibrant community where you'll meet people from diverse backgrounds and cultures, challenging your perspectives, expanding your worldview, and fostering lifelong friendships.

- **Benefit #4: Prestige and Recognition:** Attending a big-name college or university can really give your reputation a boost when you're hunting for a job. It shows employers that you're serious about your education and determined to succeed. A prestigious school name on your resume can open doors and make you stand out from other candidates, giving you an edge in a competitive job market. After all, it's not just the education you receive—it's the recognition and respect that come with it. Even if you don't attend an Ivy League school, earning a degree is a huge accomplishment that deserves recognition and respect. A college diploma can be a valuable asset in your career journey, regardless of the institution.

Cons

• **Drawback #1: Money, Money, Money:** Paying for college is a major decision for many students and their families. Here's a breakdown of the costs involved:

  • **Tuition:** This is the primary expense, covering the cost of your classes. Tuition rates can vary significantly depending on the type of institution (public vs. private), its reputation, and location.

  • **Books and Supplies:** Textbooks are often a large expense, and you may also need to purchase additional materials like digital access codes, lab manuals, or art supplies for specific courses.

  • **Room and Board:** If you plan to live on campus, factor in housing and meal costs. These can also vary based on your chosen accommodation (dorm, apartment) and the location of your college. Colleges in major cities tend to have higher living expenses.

• **Drawback #2: Navigating the Time Sink:** College life is a chaotic mix of deadlines, exams, and an ever-growing list of tasks. Juggling academics, extracurriculars, and social life is like walking a tightrope, and finding time for it all can feel impossible. With lectures, labs, and group projects consuming your days, and often nights, it's easy to resort to caffeine-fueled study sessions just to keep up. Add part-time jobs, internships, or volunteering to the equation, and the pressure intensifies, making for a truly overwhelming experience.

• **Drawback #3: Competitive Admissions:** Getting into college can, at times and at certain institutions, be a cutthroat race. With everyone vying for limited spots, good grades aren't enough. You need to excel in extracurricular activities, demonstrate community involvement, and showcase leadership qualities. Your personal essays become a crucial tool to highlight your unique personality and convince admissions officers that you're the ideal candidate. In this high-stakes environment, securing a place requires unwavering dedication, resilience, and a commitment to excellence in all areas of life, both inside and outside the classroom.

• **Drawback #4: Changing Job Market:** The job market is evolving faster than ever thanks to rapid technological advancements and automation. This means that the college degrees that were once considered gold standards might not hold the same weight anymore. With robots taking over some tasks and new technologies constantly emerging, employers are looking for candidates with up-to-date skills and the ability to adapt to changing demands, despite what college they attended. Traditional degrees are now being challenged, and there's a growing emphasis on staying ahead of the curve.

———

Is college right for you? It depends on your unique goals, finances, and what makes you tick. Consider the potential benefits – a deeper understanding of your chosen field, valuable skills, and maybe even that coveted diploma. But keep in mind, college isn't without its challenges. It requires time, money, and hard work.

The bottom line: the decision to pursue higher education should reflect your values, aspirations, and vision for the future. There's no one-size-fits-all answer, so weigh the pros and cons carefully.

CHOOSING A COLLEGE

Does It Matter Where You Go?

If you're thinking about going to college, you might be wondering, *does it really matter where I go?* It's a valid concern, especially with so many schools out there and everyone having their own take on it. Sure, going to a big-name university can have some perks, like better networking and maybe even catching the eye of some top employers. But others believe that what truly matters is your own drive, skills, and what you bring to the table.

To shed some light on this debate, we'll explore different factors to consider like academic programs, class sizes, locations, and cost. So, whether you're aiming for Ivy League status or contemplating a more unconventional path, let's navigate the terrain of college selection and find out what truly matters in the pursuit of higher education and career success.

How do you choose the right college for you? It all comes down to your goals, preferences, and priorities.

Here are a few factors to consider:

- **Academic Programs:** When thinking about where to go to college, it's important to check out the academic programs they offer. Look for schools that have majors and programs you're interested in and that can help you reach your career goals. Here's a breakdown of considerations:

Academic Programs Overview		
Interest Area	Universities	Notable Features
Computer Science	MIT, Stanford, University of Illinois	Cutting-edge research facilities, renowned professors
Engineering	Georgia Tech, Texas A&M University, Purdue University	Strong industry connections, innovative research projects
Business	University of Pennsylvania (Wharton), University of Michigan (Ross), University of Texas at Austin (McCombs)	Internship opportunities, renowned faculty
Health Sciences	Johns Hopkins University, University of California, San Francisco (UCSF), University of Washington Medical School	State-of-the-art facilities, hands-on clinical experience
Liberal Arts	Williams College, Amherst College, Swarthmore College	Diverse course offerings, emphasis on critical thinking
Environmental Science	University of Washington, University of Colorado Boulder, University of British Columbia	Research opportunities, sustainability initiatives
Hospitality Management	Cornell University, University of Nevada Las Vegas, University of Central Florida	Internship programs, industry partnerships

Education	Teachers College Columbia University, University of Pennsylvania Graduate School of Education, University of California, Los Angeles (UCLA)	Hands-on teaching experience, renowned faculty
Psychology	University of Illinois at Urbana-Champaign, University of Minnesota - Twin Cities, University of Washington	Research opportunities, diverse areas of study
Economics	Massachusetts Institute of Technology (MIT), University of Michigan - Ann Arbor, University of Virginia	Rigorous coursework, faculty expertise

These examples represent just a fraction of the diverse academic programs and opportunities out there for you to explore. Use them to kickstart your search and find the college that's the perfect fit for your interests, goals, and aspirations.

• **Class Size:** Another factor when choosing a college is class size. Smaller classes can mean more one-on-one time with professors and a better chance to really dig into the material. You'll have the opportunity to ask questions, participate in discussions, and get personalized feedback on your work. This personalized attention can lead to a more engaging and enriching learning experience overall. On the other hand, larger classes may offer a more diverse range of perspectives and experiences, as well as opportunities for group projects and collaboration. Think about your learning style and preferences when considering class sizes at different colleges.

• **Hands-on Learning:** Real-world experience is key to unlocking your post-college career path. Whether it's working at a local business, participating in a corporate co-op program, or conducting research alongside professors, hands-on learning enhances your education and equips you with valuable skills and experience. It's also an excellent way to network with professionals in your field.

When choosing a college, prioritize those that offer many hands-on opportunities aligned with your career goals. Seek out internships, co-op programs, and research projects that can give you a taste of your future profession and set you up for success.

• **Location:** Think about where you want to live and study. Are you drawn to the hustle and bustle of a big city, or do you prefer the charm of a small town? Consider factors like climate, cost of living, and proximity to family and friends. Living in a big city offers access to cultural events, internships at top companies, and diverse career opportunities, but it may come with higher living expenses and a more fast-paced lifestyle. On the other hand, studying in a small town can provide a close-knit community, lower cost of living, and a more relaxed atmosphere, but it may have fewer job prospects and cultural amenities. Think about what type of environment will best support your academic and personal growth, and choose a college location that aligns with your preferences and lifestyle.

• **Cost and Financial Aid:** College can be expensive, so it's important to evaluate your budget and financial aid options. Look for schools that offer scholarships, grants, and other forms of financial assistance to help offset the cost of tuition and expenses. From scholarships tailored to academic achievements to grants for community service endeavors, the spectrum is vast and diverse.

If you're looking for more affordable tuition rates, state or local colleges and community colleges can provide significant financial relief. And if financial aid and scholarships fall short, student loans or parent loans can help bridge the gap to fund your education.

- **Campus Culture:** Another category to consider when choosing a college is campus culture. Start by visiting different campuses (if possible) to get a feel for the culture and vibe. Do you see yourself fitting in and thriving there? Consider factors like student organizations, campus amenities, and social activities.

When you step foot on campus, take a deep breath and soak it all in. Pay attention to the little details—the laughter echoing from dorm windows, the vibrant murals adorning campus buildings, the eclectic mix of students milling about. These are the things that will give you a true sense of the culture and vibe of the campus.

———

Choosing a college is a personal journey with lots to consider, such as academic programs, location, and campus culture. While prestigious universities might seem appealing, it's ultimately about finding a place where you can thrive and make the most of your college experience. Don't let finances be a dealbreaker – explore scholarships and financial aid options that can make your dreams a reality.

CHOOSING YOUR MAJOR

Now, let's talk about choosing a major. Feeling overwhelmed? That's totally normal. Many students enter college undecided and end up discovering their passion along the way. Here's an important tip: you don't have to know your major right away. Typically, you'll declare your major by the end of your sophomore year, but some programs may require you to decide earlier. Here are a few tips to help you navigate the process.

• **Self-Reflect:** Start by reflecting on your strengths, weaknesses, and passions. If you haven't already, take the Holland Code Assessment to gain deeper insights into your interests and skills. What subjects do you love learning about? What activities make you lose track of time? Your major should align with your natural talents and interests.

Also, think about the classes you disliked in high school. If math wasn't your strong suit, steer clear of majors like engineering or finance. If biology bored you, then health sciences might not be the right fit. But if you aced history and loved learning about the past, consider exploring majors like history or political science. If English was your favorite, consider literature or journalism. Choosing a major you enjoy sets you up for a more fulfilling college experience.

• **Research Career Paths:** We learned earlier that you don't need to wait for a college degree to start working in a field you love. So you can choose your major with a career path in mind, develop your skills and education over time, and ultimately find fulfilling work. Dig deep in this research so you can make confident decisions about your major and career path–decisions that you feel great about.

• **Seek Guidance:** When it's time to nail down your major, don't be shy about seeking guidance from those who've walked the walk. This is where your *support squad* will come in handy. Also, your college likely has advisors or counselors dedicated to helping students navigate these decisions. Schedule a meeting, drop them an email, or swing by their office for a chat. They're well-versed in majors, careers, and everything you need to know to make the right choice.

By combining self-reflection, research, and guidance, you'll be well-equipped to choose a major that sets you on a fulfilling and successful path.

ALTERNATIVES TO COLLEGE

Not everyone is cut out for the traditional college experience, and that's totally okay. Fortunately, there are plenty of alternative paths to success that don't involve pursuing a four-year degree. These alternatives offer diverse opportunities for people to gain valuable skills and launch fulfilling careers. Let's explore some of these alternative paths.

- **Entrepreneurship:** Entrepreneurship is the act of building your own business from the ground up. Think about Mark Zuckerberg, the founder of Facebook—he started with an idea and a passion, just like you might. It's an exhilarating alternative to the college route, where instead of just sitting in lectures, you learn by doing and create something that's entirely yours, all while pursuing your passions. Plus, owning your own business offers a level of freedom and flexibility that's rare in a traditional job. We'll explore entrepreneurship in more detail later in the book.

- **Vocational Schools and Certification Programs:** Vocational training offers another alternative to college. These programs provide specialized training in fields like automotive repair, hairstyling, or healthcare. They focus entirely on the skills you need for your chosen job, helping you get into the workforce faster than traditional college. Employers value graduates from these programs because they're well-prepared and know what to expect. Plus, vocational programs usually cost less than regular college, which can help you avoid excessive student debt. Many of these schools also assist with job placement, offering support with resumes, interview preparation, and connecting you with potential employers after you finish.

- **Online Courses:** Digital courses are an excellent alternative to college, offering a convenient, affordable, and flexible way to learn skills and obtain certifications, regardless of where you are in your career. For example, over 100,000 professionals worldwide have become certified life coaches through online learning. Many people also teach themselves niche skills, such as how to retouch photos, by simply watching YouTube videos, mastering in-demand skills for the digital age. Additionally, there is a growing market for creating and selling online courses (projected to reach $370 billion by 2026). E-learning can also equip you with other in-demand skills like copywriting or social media marketing.

Platforms like YouTube, Coursera, and Udemy offer a wealth of options, covering a wide range of subjects. The flexibility of self-paced learning means you can learn whenever and wherever it's convenient for you. Many colleges are also embracing this trend, offering online programs that allow you to earn a degree from the comfort of your own home.

TLDR: CHARTING YOUR EDUCATIONAL PATH

We've covered a lot of ground in this chapter, diving into the different paths you can take after high school. Let's review.

- **Choosing Your Journey:** Consider your interests, finances, and learning style when deciding on an educational route. College might be the perfect fit for some, while others may thrive through different avenues.

- **Exploration and Research:** Take the time to research different career fields, academic programs, or colleges to find the best fit for your aspirations.

- **College: Just One Option:** While college offers benefits like higher earning potential and expanded career options, it's not the only road to success. Explore alternatives like entrepreneurship, vocational schools, and online courses to find the direction that aligns with your goals and interests.

- **Your Journey, Your Choice:** The decision of which direction to take is ultimately yours. Choose the one that resonates with your values, passions, and vision for the future.

Next up, we'll explore the world of career possibilities. To give you a sense of the diversity out there, get ready to dip your toes into three distinct fields: STEM, business, and the creative arts. Let's see what each one has to offer.

CHAPTER 6
DIVERSE PATHS: STEM, BUSINESS & FINANCE, AND CREATIVE CAREERS

 "Choose a job you love, and you will never have to work a day in your life."

CONFUCIUS

W hy is exploring different careers so important? Picture yourself at a massive buffet, overflowing with delicious options. You're starving, so you grab the first dessert you see – a tempting slice of chocolate cake. But as you settle down to enjoy it, you notice three even more amazing treats – crème brûlée, tiramisu, and strawberry cheese-cake. Ugh, if only you hadn't filled up on cake!

Now rewind. What if you had taken a quick look around the entire buffet before grabbing that first plate? You'd have seen all the amazing choices and could have made a more informed decision about what to try.

Career exploration is exactly like that buffet experience. The world is full of incredible career options, each with its own unique flavor and appeal. Just like with the buffet, it's wise to explore the whole spread before committing to one dish. If you take the time to learn about different career paths early on, you're more likely to find one that truly satisfies your passions and utilizes your skills.

Think of career exploration as a massive buffet, overflowing with options to satisfy any appetite. In this chapter, we'll take a tour, sampling three distinct realms: STEM, business & finance, and the arts. First, we'll check out the STEM table, where problem-solvers and innovators thrive, tackling real challenges and expanding knowledge. Next, we'll venture into the world of business and finance, where strategists and dealmakers build companies and manage money. Finally, we'll explore the vibrant creative corner, showcasing the many different possibilities for artistic careers in areas like design, music, writing, and more.

STEM CAREERS: AN OVERVIEW

Have you ever wondered how your phone works or how doctors use lasers to perform surgery? That's the power of STEM – Science, Technology, Engineering, and Mathematics – in action. STEM transcends textbooks and formulas; it's the driving force behind shaping the future.

Envision yourself collaborating with brilliant minds, tackling challenges that have a global impact. In the world of STEM, you could be the biomedical engineer designing life-changing pros-thetic limbs, the computer scientist coding the next viral app, or the astrophysicist unraveling the mysteries of the cosmos.

Why STEM?

It's not just a career, it's a calling—a chance to tackle the big problems that matter. Dream of a greener planet? STEM is powering the solutions. Want to fight diseases and make people healthier? STEM is at the forefront. Curious about the universe's secrets? STEM is unlocking those mysteries.

Beyond that, STEM careers offer the ultimate trifecta: brain-boosting challenges, competitive pay, and the security of knowing your skills will always be in demand. Plus, these fields are constantly evolving, so you'll never stop learning and growing while making a real difference in the world. Let's unpack how to get started.

Education: Building a Strong Foundation

Formal education is the launchpad for your STEM career. It equips you with the foundational knowledge and skills needed to excel in this demanding field. A bachelor's degree in areas like computer science, engineering, biology, math, or physics is often the first step towards unlocking a world of exciting opportunities.

Sharpening Your STEM Skillset

Strong academics are a great foundation, but to truly stand out in STEM fields, you'll need to build a strong set of essential skills. Here's what you'll need in your STEM toolbox:

- **Math proficiency:** especially in algebra, calculus, and statistics.

- **Scientific literacy**: in order to design experiments, analyze data, and draw conclusions.

- **Critical thinking and problem-solving**: to tackle challenges creatively.

- **Creativity and innovation:** because STEM thrives on fresh ideas.

- **Technical Skills:** These are field-specific (e.g., engineers use CAD software, programmers use coding) and will vary based on the job you pursue in STEM.

- **Soft Skills:** These include clear communication with others, a strong work ethic, and perseverance.

Getting Your Foot in the Door

If you are ready to jumpstart your STEM career, entry-level roles are your launching pad. Through internships, co-op programs, and research opportunities, you can:

- Put your classroom learning to work in the real world.
- Hone your skills through hands-on experience.
- Connect with professionals and explore various career options.
- Earn valuable references to boost your future job applications.

Here are some great entry-level positions that can give you valuable experience and open doors to many job opportunities in the future.

Entry Level Jobs

- **Research Assistants:** Work alongside scientists and researchers in labs or field projects.

- **Laboratory Technicians:** Assist with experiments, analyze data, and maintain lab equipment.

- **Software Developers (Junior)**: Help create and test software applications under the guidance of experienced developers.

- **Engineering Interns**: Gain valuable hands-on experience working on engineering projects with professional engineers.

Pros and Cons of STEM Careers

Now that you've got a game plan for building your STEM skill set, let's take a deep breath and explore the good stuff – and the not-so-good stuff – about STEM careers.

Advantages

Picture this: graduation day rolls around, you snag your dream STEM job, and companies are practically begging you to join their team. Sounds ideal, right? Well, that's the reality for many STEM professionals. Here's what a job in STEM can do for you:

- **Jobs Galore:** STEM fields are exploding with growth. These careers are some of the fastest-growing around, thanks to all the new technological advancements and the ever-increasing need for sophisticated data analysis across industries.

- **Competitive Pay:** Let's face it, financial stability is important. The good news? STEM careers often come with lucrative salaries and benefits. Because these jobs demand specialized skills and knowledge, compensation tends to be significantly higher than in many other fields.

- **Make a Difference in the World:** STEM careers empower you to make a real difference in the world. With a job in STEM, you could design sustainable energy solutions, discover cures for diseases, or invent groundbreaking technologies. STEM professionals are the heroes of the future, tackling global challenges and driving progress through innovation.

Challenges

Sure, STEM careers can be fascinating, offering opportunities that are cutting-edge and full of possibilities. But before diving in, there are a few important challenges to consider.

- **Serious Training Required:** STEM fields are known for their demanding coursework and hands-on training. Think of it like training for a marathon – it takes extreme dedication and perseverance. However, the reward, like crossing the finish line of a marathon, can be immense personal satisfaction and a fulfilling career.

- **Technology Keeps Evolving:** The world of STEM moves fast. What's considered cutting-edge today might be considered outdated tomorrow, thanks to constant advancements and changing industry needs. You will need to stay on top of the latest tech and constantly learn new skills to stay relevant in this ever-evolving field.

- **The Inclusion Challenge:** Let's be honest, STEM hasn't always been the most welcoming to everyone. Many fields are still dominated by men, which can make it tougher for women and minorities to break in. The good news? There's a big push for diversity and inclusion in STEM. While there's still work to be done, things are moving in the right direction.

The Verdict: Is STEM Your Calling?

So, is a STEM career your dream job? Here's the exciting part: STEM fields are booming, offering abundant job opportunities, competitive salaries, and the chance to make a real difference. Of course, there's always a trade-off. STEM can be demanding, requiring dedication, hard work, and continuous learning in a rapidly evolving field. By weighing all the factors, you can determine if STEM is the perfect fit for you.

BUSINESS AND FINANCE CAREERS: AN OVERVIEW

Have you ever found yourself wondering what goes on behind the scenes of the companies you love? The world of Business and Finance isn't just stuffy suits and stacks of cash. It's a vibrant ecosystem teeming with diverse career paths, each playing a crucial role in an organization's success.

CAREERS IN BUSINESS

Forget the image of a solitary accountant hunched over a desk, buried under mountains of paperwork. The reality of business and finance careers is far more exciting. Business careers are like a choose-your-own-adventure story. You're not stuck in one role; you get to explore various departments and discover the perfect fit. The path of business and finance offers a huge array of jobs to explore.

- **Accounting:** Do you have an eye for detail and a love of numbers? Accountants meticulously analyze financial data, uncovering trends and ensuring everything runs smoothly. Think of them as financial puzzle solvers, piecing together the big picture from complex data sets.

- **Marketing:** Does creativity set your soul on fire? Marketers use their creativity to develop campaigns and strategies that connect brands with their customers. They're the storytellers of the business world, weaving narratives that spark excitement and build brand loyalty.

- **Business Executives:** If you have a strategic mind and a natural ability to lead, a career as a business executive might be your calling. Business executives create winning strategies, motivate teams to achieve ambitious goals, and ultimately drive the entire organization's success.

- **Human Resources:** If you're passionate about building positive workplaces and supporting employee well-being, a career in human resources could be fulfilling. Human Resource specialists ensure employee well-being and drive a strong company culture. Think of them as the heart of the organization, keeping everything running smoothly and employees happy.

- **Operations:** Are you a master of organization and efficiency? Operations managers are the conductors of the business symphony. They ensure smooth workflows and keep the entire business running like a well-oiled machine. They're the problem-solvers behind the scenes, making sure every department hits the right note.

These are just a few examples of the many diverse and exciting career paths you can find in the business world. Whether you're passionate about people, numbers, strategy, or operations, there's a role that's perfect for you.

CAREERS IN FINANCE

Now, let's shift gears to finance, the powerhouse keeping the business world humming. Finance professionals are the strategists who analyze markets, make crucial investment decisions, and make sure companies have the resources they need to succeed.

Depending on your interests, you could pursue a career in these financial areas:

- **Corporate Finance:** Do you dream of building a company's financial future? Corporate finance strategists create winning plans that fuel growth and profitability, ensuring the company makes sound financial decisions.

- **Investment Banking:** If the idea of connecting investors with lucrative opportunities and helping to make major financial deals truly excites you, then a career in investment banking could be your calling. As an investment banker, you'll be at the forefront of high-stakes financial transactions, advising companies on mergers, acquisitions, and raising capital.

- **Financial Planners:** Do you enjoy empowering others? Financial planners guide people on the path to financial security by crafting personalized investment plans. They act as trusted advisors, helping people make smart choices with their money.

- **Risk Management:** If you have a knack for identifying and mitigating potential financial risks, a career in risk management could be a great fit. Risk management specialists are the ultimate problem-solvers in the financial world. They identify, assess, and minimize financial risks, working to prevent losses and ensure the organization's financial stability.

- **Financial Analyst:** Are you a data nerd who loves cracking codes? Financial analysts are the information sleuths of the business world, dissecting financial data to uncover trends and assess investment opportunities. They're the ones who break down financial data and share their findings, which empower businesses to make sound decisions about their money.

How to Get Started in Business and Finance Careers

Envision yourself closing those million-dollar deals, unlocking the secrets behind market trends, and staying one step ahead in the ever-changing financial scene. Sounds pretty exciting, right? But where do you even start?

Build Your Skills

The first step to starting your business and finance career is building a strong foundation of skills. This industry values people who can understand and work with numbers in specific ways, but it also goes beyond just calculations. Here are some key skills that will set you up for success:

- **Number Crunching with a Twist:** This skill goes beyond simply crunching numbers. With a career in business and finance, you'll be analyzing financial statements, market reports, and economic data to identify hidden patterns, forecast trends, and identify potential risks and rewards for investors and businesses. Think of it as financial detective work, where your analytical skills can unlock expert opinions and drive smart decision-making.

- **Communication is Key:** Numbers tell stories, but you need to be able to explain them clearly to others. Strong communication skills, both written and verbal, are essential. You'll need to present your findings and recommendations to colleagues, clients, or even investors in a way that's easy to understand, even for those who aren't finance experts.

- **Think Like a Strategist:** Business and finance involve planning for the future. You'll need to develop strong analytical and problem-solving skills. This means being able to assess different scenarios, weigh potential outcomes, and come up with creative solutions to complex challenges.

Choose Your Education Path

Your education plays a crucial role in launching your business and finance career. Start by equipping yourself with the knowledge and credentials employers seek.

- **Formal Education:** Earning a degree in business administration, finance, or economics provides a strong foundation in business and finance principles. Some universities also offer specialized degrees in areas like financial management, risk management, or international business. Consider your specific interests within the field when choosing a program.

- **Continuing Education & Certifications:** Enhance your skill set and marketability by pursuing additional education beyond your core degree. Many colleges, professional organizations, and online platforms offer courses and certifications in specialized areas. Explore options in financial planning, investment analysis, digital marketing, or data analytics depending on your career goals. These targeted programs can give you a competitive edge in the job market.

Internships and Entry-Level Positions

Just like in STEM, hands-on experience is a huge advantage for thriving business and finance professionals. Let's see how you can gain that edge.

- **Internships:** Internships are more than just resume builders. They're your chance to apply classroom knowledge in real-world settings, develop practical skills, and network with industry pros. Envision yourself assisting with financial analysis at an investment firm, or conducting market research for a major corporation. Internships give you a sneak peek into the daily grind (and the exciting wins) of various business and finance roles, helping you chart your perfect career path.

- **Entry-Level Positions:** Entry-level roles are your springboard into the industry. Just think–you can start out as a financial analyst, marketing coordinator, or administrative assistant, and you'll gain valuable on-the-job experience to build a strong foundation for your future success.

A successful business and finance career is built on a trifecta: education, skills, and experience. By pursuing the right academic path, mastering key skills, and diving into internships and entry-level roles, you're laying the groundwork for a fulfilling and exciting quest in this dynamic field.

Pros and Cons of Business and Finance Careers

The world of Business and Finance isn't all numbers and board-rooms. It's a dynamic blend of opportunity and challenge. Let's explore the flip sides of the coin.

Pros: Unlock Your Potential

- **High Earning Potential:** Business and Finance can be a lucrative path. You'll earn a competitive salary with opportunities for advancement, all rewards for the specialized skills you bring to the table. Investment banking, corporate finance, and financial planning are some of the business and finance fields that can come with very attractive compensation packages.

- **A World of Possibilities:** Variety is the spice of life, and Business and Finance offers a smorgasbord of career options. This field welcomes financial analysts, investment bankers, financial advisors, risk managers – and anyone with the passion and skills to thrive. So, if you love crunching numbers or crafting strategic plans, this is the field for you.

- **Lifelong Learning:** The business world is constantly evolving, and so are the skills you'll use. This field offers endless opportunities for growth and development. Master new technologies, adapt to market trends, and expand your network – there's always a new challenge to conquer.

Cons: Navigate the Grind

- **Pressure Cooker Environment:** The business and finance world can be a pressure cooker. If you choose this path, be ready to tackle tight deadlines, fierce competition, and high stakes, which can lead to stress and burnout.

- **Work-Life Balance?:** Long hours are often the norm in business and finance. Meeting deadlines and market demands can mean evenings, weekends, and even holidays dedicated to work. This demanding schedule requires a strong work ethic and dedication, but it can also impact your personal life.

- **Market Mayhem:** The world of finance is constantly in flux. Market fluctuations, economic shifts – these are all part of the game. Business and finance professionals need to be adaptable, make informed decisions, and navigate uncertainty with confidence.

Is It Right for You?

Business and Finance offers a wealth of opportunities for those who are passionate, strategic, and innovative. From high earning potential to diverse career paths and continuous learning, the rewards are undeniable. However, it's crucial to be aware of the challenges – the stress, long hours, and ever-changing landscape. Weighing all the options will help you make a smart choice and be ready for anything the industry throws your way.

CREATIVE CAREERS: AN OVERVIEW

Set aside your spreadsheets and business plans for a moment. This section is all about the incredible world of the arts. The arts offer a chance to create something you're proud of, to express yourself in a whole new way. It's a truly unique career path.

- **Art and Design:** Have you ever imagined seeing your artwork hanging in a museum, or designing the next eye-catching ad campaign? That's the world of art and design. It's not just paintbrushes and clay anymore. These days, artists and designers use all sorts of tools, from computers to tablets, to create amazing work. From classic paintings and sculptures to mind-blowing digital art and animations, this field lets you unleash your creativity in a variety of ways. With a career in art and design, you could be showcasing your work in galleries and museums. Or, you could help design everything from websites to movie posters at advertising agencies and design studios.

- **Music:** Think of yourself in a recording studio, pouring your heart out through your music, your voice filling the room with raw emotion. Or perhaps you envision yourself as a seasoned music teacher, guiding a student through their first chords and watching their passion for music ignite. Maybe you see yourself as a sound engineer, meticulously adjusting levels, ensuring every note sounds perfect. These are just a few of the many exciting possibilities that await you in the vibrant world of music careers. As a musician, you have the power to move people, to tell stories, and to create something truly unique. Lay down your own tracks as a recording artist, collaborate with other musicians as a session player, or nurture the next generation of musicians as a music educator. You could even dive into the technical side of things as an audio technician, crafting the perfect soundscapes that bring music to life.

- **Writing:** Remember that captivating novel that transported you to another world, or the powerful news article that exposed injustice and sparked change? Those are the fingerprints of writers, individuals who wield words to shape minds and touch hearts. Writers have the power to transport readers to distant lands, challenge their perspectives, and spark their imaginations. Whether you aspire to craft bestselling novels, expose hidden truths as a journalist, or create captivating scripts for the screen, a writing career offers diverse paths for self-expression and influence.

- **Film:** Ever find yourself on the edge of your seat during a thriller, or laughing until your sides hurt at a comedy? That's the power of film – using visuals and sound to transport us to different worlds, evoke emotions, and tell unforgettable stories. You could be making independent films, crafting thought-provoking documentaries, or even working on the next Hollywood blockbuster. It's a collaborative effort, where creativity and technical skill combine to create magic on the silver screen. And with the industry constantly evolving, there's always something new and exciting to explore.

Creative careers provide countless opportunities to unleash your imagination, express your unique perspective, and make a lasting impact through art, music, writing, and film. These professions offer fulfilling avenues for self-expression and creativity, allowing you to leave your mark on the world.

Launching Your Creative Career

The creative world is a vibrant mix of artistic talent, technical know-how, and a go-getter attitude. Whether you're drawn to music, writing, film, or the visual arts, there's a path for you. Let's explore the skills and tools you'll need to bring your creative vision to life.

Technical Skills

- **Mastering the Design Toolbox:** You've probably heard of Adobe Photoshop or Illustrator. These are just a few programs you'll use to create amazing visuals. Dive into 3D modeling with Maya or Blender to take your skills to new heights.

- **Becoming a DAW Master:** What if you could transform your bedroom into a recording studio? With DAWs (Digital Audio Workstations) like Ableton Live or Logic Pro, it's possible. Learning how to use a DAW will give you the skills you need to compose, arrange, and produce your own music.

- **Editing Like a Pro:** Dream of being the next Spielberg? Mastering video editing software like Adobe Premiere Pro or Final Cut Pro is a crucial step. Combine that with camera skills and an understanding of film production, and you'll be well on your way to a career on set.

- **Writing & Content Creation Powerhouse:** Got a way with words? Honing your communication skills is essential. If you're into online content, learning website platforms like WordPress and SEO techniques will help your work reach a wider audience.

The information I'm sharing covers general technical skills you might need, but the exact skills can vary depending on your specific creative path.

Soft Skills for Creativity

Technical skills are important, but don't overlook the power of soft skills in the creative arts. These are the interpersonal strengths that can make or break a project, a collaboration, or even a career. Think of it like this: you're a brilliant painter, but if you can't communicate your vision to a client or work effectively with a gallery owner, your masterpiece might never see the light of day.

- **Lifelong Curiosity:** Embrace the spirit of lifelong curiosity, a constant thirst for knowledge and inspiration that fuels your creativity. Actively seek out different art forms and cultures. With a lifelong curiosity, you will broaden your perspectives, spark creative connections, and always stay inspired.

- **Embrace Experimentation:** Don't be afraid to experiment and learn from mistakes. It's where you can break free from the confines of perfectionism and discover new ideas, techniques, and possibilities. You don't need to be perfect; instead, challenge yourself to foster creativity.

- **Communication:** Hone your written and verbal communication skills. You'll need to clearly express your ideas, collaborate with others, and give and receive constructive feedback. Your ability to articulate your vision clearly and persuasively can make all the difference in pitching work to clients.

- **Collaboration:** Collaboration is key in the creative world. Creating extraordinary work often requires a symphony of diverse perspectives and talents working together. Be a team player who actively listens, respects different viewpoints, and contributes your unique strengths to achieve a shared vision.

- **Problem-Solving:** Unexpected challenges are part of the creative process. Develop your problem-solving skills to find creative solutions and overcome obstacles. Remember that time you faced a creative block? The ability to think outside the box and find innovative solutions is a key trait of successful creatives. Embrace the mindset that everything is solvable, because with the right approach, even the most daunting obstacles can be overcome.

- **Adaptability:** The creative landscape is constantly evolving. Be adaptable and open to learning new things to stay relevant and thrive in a changing environment. Embrace change, be open to learning new technologies and techniques, and evolve your skills to stay ahead of the curve.

- **Time Management:** Juggling multiple projects and deadlines is a reality in the creative world. Develop strong time management skills to prioritize tasks, meet deadlines, and maintain a healthy work-life balance.

Once you master these soft skills, you'll be well-equipped to collaborate effectively and thrive in the dynamic world of creative careers.

Formal Education

The creative path is unique for everyone, but a solid foundation in your chosen field is essential. Formal education can be an excellent starting point, offering several advantages.

Consider a degree program like a Bachelor of Fine Arts (BFA) as a deep dive into your artistic passion. You'll receive hands-on training from experienced professionals, experiment with various techniques and styles, and gain valuable feedback to refine your skills. It's like an immersive creative training ground where you'll not only hone your craft but also build lasting relationships with fellow artists and mentors.

Plus, formal education provides a structured environment for collaboration, where you'll team up with classmates on projects, further developing your teamwork and communication skills – essential assets in the collaborative world of creative careers.

Building a Portfolio and Finding Freelance Opportunities

Think of your portfolio as your personal spotlight, a curated collection of your best and brightest work that shines a light on your unique talents and skills. Whether you're a visual artist, musician, writer, or any other type of creative, a killer portfolio is your chance to make a lasting impression on potential clients and employers. Showcase your most impressive projects, demonstrating your range and versatility. Add captions that tell the story behind each piece, highlighting your role and the impact you made. Don't forget to sprinkle in those glowing testimonials from satisfied clients – they're like gold stars for your creative resume.

But a stellar portfolio is just the first step. In the creative world, networking is key. Platforms like Upwork can connect you with freelance gigs that match your expertise. Social media is your virtual stage – use it to showcase your work, engage with fellow creatives, and build a loyal following. And don't forget the power of real-world connections. Attend industry events, join professional organizations, and never miss an opportunity to mingle with like-minded individuals. By expanding your network, you will open many doors to new and fulfilling opportunities.

By mastering your craft, showcasing your talent, and actively seeking opportunities, you're paving the way for a fulfilling and successful creative career. There will be challenges, but the journey of turning your passion into reality is an incredibly rewarding one.

Pros and Cons of Creative Careers

Creative careers offer a tremendous amount of fulfillment for those driven by the arts However, like any career path, there are both advantages and challenges to consider. Let's explore the rewards and drawbacks of pursuing a career in the creative industries.

Advantages

- **Freedom & Flexibility:** Creative careers often offer the autonomy to choose projects, set your own schedule, and work from anywhere. Ever daydream about what it would be like to design from a beach hammock or even write your next masterpiece in a Parisian café? This flexibility allows you to tailor your work to your life and pursue projects that truly ignite your passion.

- **Fulfillment & Satisfaction:** There's a unique sense of accomplishment that comes from using your talents to create something meaningful. Captivating artwork, heart-wrenching songs, or stories that move people – creative professionals get to share their vision with the world.

- **Collaboration & Growth:** The creative world thrives on collaboration. You'll have the chance to work with other talented artists, designers, and creatives, fostering a sense of community and camaraderie. Plus, the dynamic nature of the industry encourages continuous learning and experimentation, helping you hone your skills and grow as an artist.

Challenges

- **Financial Fluctuations:** One of the biggest hurdles in creative careers can be the inconsistent income. Freelance or project-based work can mean periods of feast or famine, requiring careful budgeting and financial planning.

- **Self-Motivation & Discipline:** Working creatively requires a high level of self-motivation and discipline. You'll need to be a self-starter who can stay focused and productive even when faced with setbacks or creative blocks. Mastering time management and perseverance are key to success in this fast-paced world.

- **Rejection and Criticism:** The subjective nature of creative work means not everything you produce will resonate with everyone. Criticism, rejection, and creative differences are part of the territory. However, learning from these experiences and maintaining a positive mindset are crucial for navigating these challenges and continuing to grow as an artist.

Creative careers present a unique combination of freedom, personal satisfaction, and challenges. Financial instability and self-doubt can be obstacles, but the rewards can be highly motivating. By focusing on your creative goals, overcoming challenges, and staying true to your artistic vision, you can build a fulfilling and rewarding career in the creative field. If you're passionate about creating, these paths offer a chance to contribute your talents and make a difference.

TLDR: EXPLORING DIVERSE CAREER PATHS

We've just scratched the surface of the incredible career options out there, and I hope you're feeling inspired. Let's recap the three main areas we explored:

- **STEM Careers:** The STEM world is all about innovation and problem-solving, tackling global challenges, and shaping the future. These careers pay well and offer job security, but be prepared for a fast-paced environment that requires constant learning.

- **Business and Finance Careers:** Business and finance professionals are the driving force behind economic growth and organizational success. Think big salaries, diverse opportunities, and the chance to make a real impact on companies and the economy. Just be ready for some long hours and high-pressure situations.

- **Creative Careers:** In the creative field, you can unleash your imagination and express yourself through art, music, writing, or film. These careers offer freedom and fulfillment, but navigating financial instability and self-doubt requires resilience and self-motivation.

Finding a career that sparks your passion and uses your skills is totally possible. And if you're dreaming even bigger, the next chapter is for you. In the following pages, we'll uncover the secrets of successful entrepreneurs and how you can pave the way to becoming your own boss. Excited yet?

See you on the other side.

CHAPTER 7
BE YOUR OWN BOSS: ENTREPRENEURSHIP

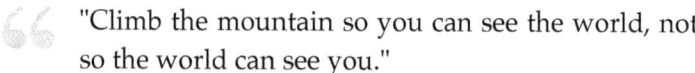

"Climb the mountain so you can see the world, not so the world can see you."

DAVID MCCULLOUGH JR.

Ever catch yourself daydreaming about being the next Mark Zuckerberg or Elon Musk, calling the shots and building your own empire? Young entrepreneurs are everywhere these days, shaking things up and inspiring a whole generation to rethink the traditional career path. They're proving you don't need a corner office to make a major impact. But is entrepreneurial life really all it's cracked up to be? Let's take a closer look at the excitement and challenges of being your own boss.

WHAT IS ENTREPRENEURSHIP?

Entrepreneurship empowers you to take the reins of your own destiny. Picture waking up every morning with the thrill of knowing that you're in charge. No more following someone else's blueprint or adhering to strict guidelines. No one telling you where to work, when to work, or what to do for work. Instead, you have the creative freedom to design, innovate, and construct a business that reflects your unique ideas and aspirations.

In essence, it's the process of starting and running your own business—identifying opportunities, taking risks, and transforming your ideas into successful ventures.

WHY ENTREPRENEURSHIP?

The allure of entrepreneurship is a powerful force, drawing people from all walks of life to pursue their dreams of building something from nothing. The reasons for taking this leap are as diverse as the entrepreneurs themselves. Let's delve deeper into some of the most common motivations that inspire people to create their own businesses.

1. The Magnetic Pull of Autonomy and Freedom: Entrepreneurship is a powerful expression of autonomy, a path for those who crave the freedom to chart their own course. You're not bound by the confines of a traditional job or corporate structure. Instead, you have the flexibility to work on your terms, taking on projects that align with your passions. Entrepreneurship is about living a life of purpose and fulfillment, having the courage to take risks, and making a meaningful impact on the world.

This freedom extends beyond just setting your own schedule and working from anywhere; it gives you the autonomy to:

- **Make your own decisions:** You're the captain of your ship, steering it in the direction you choose. You decide what products or services to offer, how to market them, and how to run your operations.

- **Create your own rules:** You're not bound by corporate policies or procedures. You can create a workplace culture that reflects your values and fosters creativity and innovation.

- **Choose your own team:** You have the power to assemble a team of talented people who share your vision and are committed to your company's success.

- **Set your own goals:** You define what success means for your business and strive to achieve your own unique objectives.

2. The Desire for Impact and Innovation: Entrepreneurship also offers the opportunity to make a tangible impact on the world. Whether you're addressing a pressing need in your community or introducing a revolutionary product to the market, being an entrepreneur allows you to leave a lasting imprint. As an entrepreneur, you can create meaningful change and contribute to something bigger than yourself.

This desire for impact can manifest in various ways:

- **Solving problems:** Entrepreneurs are often driven by a passion for solving problems, whether it's creating a product that simplifies people's lives or developing a service that addresses a social issue.

- **Creating jobs:** Successful entrepreneurs not only create opportunities for themselves but also for others. They build companies that employ people and contribute to the economy.

- **Driving innovation:** Entrepreneurs are constantly pushing the boundaries of what's possible. They introduce new products, services, and technologies that change the way we live and work.

3. The Pursuit of Personal and Professional Growth: Finally, starting and running your own business is a journey of personal and professional growth. It's a masterclass in self-improvement, cleverly disguised as a business venture. The challenges you face as an entrepreneur will push you to develop resilience, resourcefulness, and a growth mindset.

You'll grow by:

- **Developing new skills:** As an entrepreneur, you'll constantly be learning new things, from marketing and sales to finance and operations.

- **Building resilience:** Starting a business is not easy. You'll face setbacks and failures along the way. But each challenge is an opportunity to learn and grow stronger.

- **Expanding your network:** Entrepreneurs thrive on building relationships. You'll meet a wide range of people, from customers and suppliers to mentors and investors. These connections can be invaluable as you grow your business.

GETTING STARTED WITH A BUSINESS

So, you're ready to take the plunge into entrepreneurship and start your own business. The prospect is exciting, but where do you even begin? Let's break down the process into manageable steps, guiding you from that initial spark of an idea to the exhilarating moment of unveiling your venture.

Step 1: Unearthing Your Brilliant Idea

Every successful business starts with a great idea – a solution to a problem, a product people crave, or a service that fills a gap in the market. But great ideas don't just appear out of thin air; they often come from a place of passion and personal experience. What are you passionate about? What problems have you encountered in your own life that you wish someone would solve?

Brainstorming is a powerful tool for generating ideas. Grab a notebook, gather a group of friends, or simply let your mind wander. There are no bad ideas at this stage, so let your creativity flow freely. Don't be afraid to combine seemingly unrelated concepts or explore unconventional solutions.

Research is another essential component of idea generation. Dive into market trends, analyze competitor offerings, and talk to potential customers to get a sense of what they need and want. This will help you refine your idea and ensure that there's a viable market for it.

Step 2: Crafting Your Business Blueprint: The Business Plan

Think of your business plan as a detailed architectural drawing for your entrepreneurial vision. It's a comprehensive outline of your strategy, financial projections, and operational structure, providing a clear direction for your business and helping you secure the resources you need to thrive.

Your business plan should include the following key components:

- **Executive Summary:** A concise overview of your business concept, goals, and target market.

- **Company Description:** A more in-depth look at your

business, including its legal structure, products or services, mission, vision, and unique value proposition.

- **Market Analysis:** A thorough assessment of your target market, including demographics, needs, preferences, and buying behavior. This will help you understand your potential customers and tailor your offerings to meet their needs.

- **Marketing and Sales Strategy:** A detailed plan for how you'll reach and attract customers, including your marketing channels (social media, advertising, etc.), pricing strategy, and sales goals.

- **Management and Operations:** An overview of your team's structure, roles, and responsibilities, as well as your plans for day-to-day operations, production, and customer service.

- **Financial Projections:** A realistic forecast of your revenue, expenses, and cash flow over the next few years. This will demonstrate the financial viability of your business to potential investors or lenders.

Keep in mind that your business plan is not set in stone. It's a living document that will evolve as your business grows and changes.

Step 3: Making It Official: Registering Your Business

Before you can start operating legally, you need to register your business with the appropriate authorities and choose a legal structure. The most common structures include:

- **Sole Proprietorship:** The simplest structure, where you are the sole owner and are personally liable for all debts and liabilities.

- **Partnership:** A business owned by two or more people who share profits and losses.

- **Limited Liability Company (LLC):** A hybrid structure that offers the liability protection of a corporation with the tax benefits of a partnership.

- **Corporation:** A separate legal entity from its owners, offering limited liability but with more complex regulations and tax requirements.

The right legal structure for you will depend on your specific circumstances and goals. Consult with a legal professional to determine the best option for your business.

Step 4: Securing Your Financial Fuel: Finding Funding

Starting a business often requires capital to cover expenses like equipment, inventory, and marketing. There are various funding options available, each with its own advantages and disadvantages:

- **Bootstrapping:** Using your own savings or funds from friends and family. This gives you complete control but can be risky if you don't have sufficient funds.

- **Small Business Loans:** Borrowing money from a bank or other financial institution. This can provide the necessary capital but requires a solid business plan and credit history.

- **Angel Investors:** Wealthy individuals who invest in early-stage companies in exchange for equity. They can provide funding and valuable mentorship but may require giving up a portion of ownership. Think *Shark Tank*, but in real life.

- **Venture Capital:** Firms that invest in high-growth potential companies in exchange for equity. They can provide significant funding but have high expectations for returns.

- **Crowdfunding:** Raising funds from a large number of people online, often through platforms like Kickstarter or Indiegogo. This can be a great way to generate buzz, validate your idea, and build a community of early adopters around your product or service. However, it requires a compelling pitch and a strong marketing strategy to attract and engage potential backers.

Your business plan will be a critical tool in securing funding. Investors and lenders want to see that you have a clear vision, a solid strategy, and a realistic financial plan.

Step 5: Unveiling Your Creation: Launching Your Business

With your plan in place and funding secured, it's time to unleash your business upon the world. This is where all your hard work and preparation culminate in the exciting launch of your venture.

The launch phase can look different for each business. It might involve setting up a website, opening a physical store, creating a buzz on social media, or running targeted advertising campaigns. The key is to tailor your launch strategy to your target market and your unique value proposition.

During the launch phase, it's crucial to stay flexible and adaptable. Things may not always go according to plan, so be prepared to adjust your strategy as needed. Continuously gather feedback from customers, track your progress, and make necessary changes to ensure your business thrives.

Building a successful business is a journey of unwavering dedication, resilience, and continuous learning. Embrace the process with patience and focus, and your entrepreneurial vision will become a reality.

SKILLS YOU'LL NEED FOR ENTREPRENEURSHIP

Embarking on the path of entrepreneurship takes more than a brilliant idea and a dash of risk-taking spirit. It demands a toolkit of skills to navigate challenges and seize opportunities. Let's explore these essential skills, drawing inspiration from some incredibly accomplished people who have achieved their dreams.

Leadership: Lilly Singh

Being an entrepreneur is not about being the boss, it's about being a leader – inspiring and guiding your team, your employees, and even your customers toward a shared vision for your business. Look at Lilly Singh, the multi-talented comedian and entrepreneur formerly known as Superwoman. Her success stems not only from her comedic talent, but from her ability to connect with and empower her audience through infectious energy and determination. Singh's philosophy of putting her all into everything, whether it's refilling forks at a cafe or auditioning for a role, demonstrates a work ethic and dedication that have made her a leader in the entertainment industry.

As you embark on your entrepreneurial journey, consider how you can emulate Singh's leadership style. How can you inspire and motivate your team, create a culture of empowerment, and connect with customers on a personal level?

Problem-Solving: LeBron James

Every entrepreneur faces challenges, from unexpected setbacks to logistical hurdles. But, like NBA legend LeBron James, you can turn those challenges into stepping stones. As a young boy facing poverty and instability, James and his mother moved numerous times, leading to missed school days and a constant sense of upheaval. However, when they finally found a home in the Spring Hill apartments in Akron, Ohio, it became a catalyst for his future.

The stability James found there inspired him to co-found Spring-Hill Entertainment later in life, which has grown into a major player in Hollywood, producing films like *Space Jam 2* and documentaries like *What's My Name: Muhammad Ali*, proving that he's not just a basketball player but a visionary entrepreneur.

James' story is a powerful reminder that challenges are not roadblocks, but rather opportunities for growth and innovation. By embracing a problem-solving approach, entrepreneurs can turn adversity into advantage and achieve remarkable success in their ventures. Ultimately, great leaders aren't defined solely by their ideas but by their ability to overcome obstacles through critical thinking and creative problem-solving.

Financial Literacy: Elon Musk

Financial literacy is the cornerstone of smart decision-making and sustainable growth in the entrepreneurial world. Take Elon Musk, for example, the world's wealthiest person, worth $256 billion. His journey to success wasn't simply handed to him; it was fueled by his financial expertise, developed through early business ventures and a thirst for knowledge. Musk's accomplishments with PayPal, Tesla, and SpaceX highlight the importance of understanding financial principles and using them strategically to transform innovative ideas into reality.

Here's what we can learn from Musk's journey:

1. **Focus on impact:** While financial success is a byproduct, the core motivation behind Musk's ventures has been a desire to make a meaningful difference in the world. His companies aim to solve global challenges and create a better future. When you're passionate about the problem your business is solving or the value it brings to the world, you'll be more inspired to persevere through challenges and achieve long-term success.

2. **An Unwavering Investment in Skills:** Musk consistently invests in his knowledge, skills, and businesses, even when faced with setbacks. This relentless pursuit of self-improvement and unwavering dedication to his ventures is a testament to the power of continuous learning and the importance of investing in yourself and your dreams.

3. **Mastery of Financial Principles:** Musk's success in securing funding for ambitious projects like Tesla and SpaceX demonstrates his deep understanding of financial principles. He meticulously crafted comprehensive business plans, outlining his vision, strategy, and financial projections, which helped him attract investors and secure the resources needed to bring his ideas to life.

By investing in your financial education, you're not just learning about numbers; you're empowering yourself to make sound decisions, build a sustainable business, and ultimately achieve your entrepreneurial dreams.

Adaptability: Arnold Schwarzenegger

In the fast-paced, ever-evolving business world, adaptability isn't just a valuable skill—it's a survival instinct. The ability to pivot, embrace change, and learn new things is what separates thriving entrepreneurs from those who get left behind. Just ask

Arnold Schwarzenegger, who didn't just dominate one field, but three.

Schwarzenegger's journey is a testament to the power of adaptability. He started as a bodybuilder, sculpting his physique into a work of art that earned him multiple Mr. Olympia titles. But he didn't stop there. He leveraged his charisma and determination to conquer Hollywood, becoming one of the biggest action stars of his generation. And as if that wasn't enough, he then transitioned into politics, serving as the Governor of California.

Each of these career pivots demanded that Schwarzenegger acquire new skills, embrace different mindsets, and adapt to entirely new environments. He didn't shy away from challenges; he embraced them, learning and growing with each new endeavor.

Just like Schwarzenegger, you too, as an entrepreneur, must be willing to constantly adapt and evolve. The business landscape is a whirlwind of change, with new technologies, market trends, and consumer preferences constantly emerging. To stay ahead of the curve, you need to be agile, open-minded, and ready to embrace new ideas and approaches.

BEYOND SKILLS: CONNECTIONS AND EXPERIENCE

While a great business idea and the skills to run it are essential, they're just the first steps on your career journey. The real key to success often lies in your connections and real-world experience.

Your network – the people you know and who know you – can open doors to opportunities you might not even know existed. They can offer advice, mentorship, funding, and even partnerships. And real-world experience, whether gained through internships, part-time jobs, or volunteering, gives you the practical skills and know-how that no classroom can teach.

TLDR: THE ENTREPRENEURIAL SPIRIT

In this chapter, we've explored what it means to be your own boss and why it's such an appealing path for many. Here's a quick recap of the key takeaways:

- **Understanding Entrepreneurship:** Entrepreneurship is more than just starting a business; it's a mindset, a lifestyle, and a journey of personal and professional growth. It's about taking control of your destiny, pursuing your passions, and making a meaningful impact on the world.

- **The Five Steps to Launching a Business:** We outlined the essential steps involved in starting a business, from generating ideas and crafting a business plan to securing funding and launching your venture.

- **Essential Skills for Entrepreneurial Success:** We discussed the critical skills needed to thrive as an entrepreneur, drawing inspiration from the success stories of Lilly Singh, LeBron James, Elon Musk, and Arnold Schwarzenegger. These skills include leadership, problem-solving, financial literacy, and adaptability.

Remember, entrepreneurship is a journey, not a destination. It requires hard work, dedication, and a willingness to take risks. But for those who are driven by a passion for creating something new and making a difference, it can be an incredibly rewarding path.

In the next chapter, we'll take a look at how to cultivate meaningful connections and gain hands-on experience that will catapult your business or career to success.

CHAPTER 8
NETWORKING AND REAL-WORLD EXPOSURE

 "Opportunities don't happen, you create them."

CHRIS GROSSER

oes it ever bother you to see how some people seem to effortlessly glide through life, doors swinging open before them on every turn? While it may appear to be pure luck, the truth is, nothing happens by chance.

In fact, studies have shown that a significant portion of job opportunities are never even advertised, instead being filled through personal connections and referrals. Mind blowing, right? The power behind this phenomenon is networking – the art of building relationships and connecting with the right people.

So while your skills, education, and training are undoubtedly important, landing your dream job often depends on the people you connect with and the doors they can open for you.

In this chapter, I'll teach you how to build meaningful relationships, attend career fairs, and seek out real-world experiences. Together, we'll discover how to position yourself for success in the ever-evolving world of work.

WHY ATTEND CAREER FAIRS?

You may be wondering if career fairs are worth your time. Are they just a bunch of booths and brochures, or do they actually offer valuable opportunities? Here's the thing: career fairs aren't just about snagging freebies. They're your chance to connect with potential employers, discover hidden job openings, and get a feel for the companies that you absolutely love. In a nutshell, they're a one-stop shop for jumpstarting your professional journey.

NETWORKING & LANDING JOB OPPORTUNITIES AT CAREER FAIRS

Career fairs take networking to a whole new level. You can bypass the formal emails and awkward LinkedIn messages and instead engage in genuine conversations with recruiters. It's your chance to make a real connection and leave a lasting impression. You'll be able to showcase your personality, make a memorable impression, and demonstrate your passion for their company.

Think of it like a first date, but for your career. You'll have the chance to ask questions, get the inside scoop on company culture, and discover exciting career opportunities. This first-hand knowledge is invaluable and can help you tailor your job search strategy. (In fact, I landed my very first teaching job at a career fair, and two decades later, I'm still happily teaching at that same school!). Don't underestimate the potential of these events.

Even if you're not actively seeking a new job, career fairs offer numerous benefits:

- **Discover hidden opportunities:** Many companies showcase unadvertised positions at career fairs, giving you access to jobs you might not find online.

- **Learn about different industries:** Gain a broader understanding of various industries and potential career paths.

- **Practice your networking skills:** Hone your communication and interpersonal skills in a low-pressure environment.

- **Build your professional network:** Make connections that could open doors to future opportunities.

Don't discount the power of career fairs, whether you're actively job hunting or simply exploring your options. They're a chance to discover, learn, connect, and potentially secure a fulfilling career.

PREPARING FOR A CAREER FAIR

Career fairs are your express pass to connect with potential employers, but arriving unprepared is like showing up to a party without knowing anyone – awkward. To truly shine and make the most of this opportunity, it's important to strategize and prepare yourself for a successful experience.

Pack Your Resume

Think of your resume as your professional calling card—your first impression on paper. Make sure you have plenty of copies ready to hand out to recruiters. But don't just bring any old resume; tailor each one to highlight the specific skills and experiences that align with the companies you're targeting. It's like having different outfits for different occasions – you want to dress your resume to impress each potential employer.

And presentation matters. A sleek folder or portfolio not only keeps your resumes crisp and organized but also adds a touch of professionalism that shows you're serious about your career.

Dress the Part

First impressions are important, and what you wear to a career fair can speak volumes before you even utter a word. Dressing professionally signals that you're serious about your career and respectful of the opportunity. But what exactly does *professional* mean? It can vary depending on the industry you're interested in.

If you're aiming for a corporate environment, a suit or business attire (think a blazer and dress pants or a skirt) is usually a safe bet. But if you're interested in a more creative field, you might have a bit more flexibility. A polished ensemble that reflects your personal style while still looking put-together is perfectly acceptable. The goal when you're *dressing the part* is to look confident and put-together. When you feel good about your appearance, it shows in your body language and interactions

Master Your Elevator Pitch: Your 30-Second Spotlight

Imagine stepping into an elevator with a top recruiter from your dream company. You have just a few floors to make an unforgettable impression. That's where your elevator pitch comes in – your 30-second commercial for your career.

Your elevator pitch is more than just a brief introduction; it's a compelling snapshot of your unique value proposition. It should answer three key questions:

- **Who are you?** Briefly state your name and current position or field of study.

- **What do you do?** Highlight your most relevant skills, experiences, and accomplishments.

- **What are your goals?** Concisely express your career aspirations and how you can contribute to the company.

Here's a sample elevator pitch structure:

Hi, I'm [Your Name]. I'm a [Your Current Position/Field of Study] with a passion for [Your Area of Expertise]. In my previous role at [Previous Company/Project], I [Your Key Accomplishment]. I'm excited about the opportunity to [Your Career Goal] and believe my skills in [Your Skills] would be a valuable asset to your team.

Don't be afraid to inject your personality into your pitch. Let your enthusiasm and passion shine through. The goal here is to pique the recruiter's interest and leave them wanting to learn more.

Practice your elevator pitch in front of a mirror, with friends, or even record yourself. The more you practice, the more natural and confident you'll sound when the moment arrives.

Do Your Research

Knowledge is power, especially at a career fair. Before you step foot inside, take the time to research the companies that will be attending. Don't just skim their websites; dig deeper to understand their mission, values, and recent achievements. What problems are they trying to solve? What impact are they making in the world? What are their core values, and do they align with yours?

Here are some specific areas to research:

- **Company Mission and Values:** What is the company's purpose? What problems are they trying to solve? What do they value in their employees?

- **Products and Services:** What does the company offer? What are their flagship products or services? What makes them unique?

- **Recent News and Achievements:** Has the company been in the news lately? Have they received any awards or recognition? What are their latest projects or initiatives?

- **Company Culture:** What's the work environment like? What kind of people thrive at the company? How does the company support employee growth and development?

- **Open Positions:** Are there any specific job openings you're interested in? What are the qualifications and requirements?

By taking the time to research companies beforehand, you'll be making a small investment of time that can pay off big in terms of securing that perfect job. You'll be prepared to engage recruiters in meaningful conversations, ask insightful questions, and demonstrate a genuine interest in their company, leaving them thinking, "Wow, this person really did their homework!"

Polish Your Online Presence: Your Digital First Impression

In the digital age, your online presence is an extension of your professional brand. Think of your LinkedIn profile as your virtual resume, a snapshot of your skills, experience, and career aspirations. Before you hit the career fair, give your LinkedIn profile a thorough makeover. Ensure your information is up-to-date, your photo is professional, and your summary highlights your unique strengths and accomplishments.

But your LinkedIn profile is just the tip of the iceberg. Potential employers are likely to Google you, so it's crucial to review your other social media accounts. Make sure your Facebook, Twitter, Instagram, or any other platforms you use are free of any content that might raise red flags. This means removing any unprofessional photos, posts, or comments that could reflect poorly on your character or judgment. You want your online presence to reinforce the positive impression you make in person, not detract from it.

Consider it a digital detox for your career. Take the time to curate an online presence that reflects your best self – professional, polished, and ready to take on the working world.

Practice Professionalism: Your Interactions Speak Volumes

At a career fair, you're not just showcasing your skills and experience; you're representing yourself as a potential employee and future colleague. Every interaction, from the moment you step into the venue to the follow-up emails you send, is an opportunity to demonstrate your professionalism and leave a positive impression.

Your demeanor matters. Offer a firm handshake when introducing yourself – it's a classic sign of confidence and respect. Maintain eye contact during conversations to show you're engaged and attentive. Actively listen to what the recruiters and company representatives have to say, asking thoughtful questions that demonstrate your genuine interest in their organization and the role.

Keep in mind that you're not just selling yourself, you're also building relationships. Show genuine curiosity about the company's culture, values, and goals. Ask about their current projects or challenges, and offer your insights or perspectives where relevant.

After the career fair, don't forget to follow up. Send personalized thank-you emails to the recruiters and company representatives you connected with, expressing your appreciation for their time and reiterating your interest in the position. A well-crafted follow-up email can solidify your impression and keep you top of mind for potential opportunities.

NETWORKING OUTSIDE CAREER FAIRS

Beyond the structured environment of career fairs, you can find networking opportunities everywhere. In this section, we'll uncover where, why, and how you can foster meaningful connections and build relationships that open doors to your dream career.

The Power of Professional Networking

It's not just about schmoozing and exchanging business cards. Networking allows you to tap into the hidden job market, fast-track your career progression, and even spark personal growth. In today's interconnected world, nurturing meaningful relationships can seriously boost your chances of success.

Your networking opportunities aren't confined to just career fairs. While those events are an excellent starting point, they're just one piece of the networking puzzle. Think of them as speed dating for your career – a whirlwind of brief introductions. To truly reap the benefits of networking, you need to go beyond those initial sparks and cultivate deeper, lasting connections. Let's take a look at where to make those connections.

Digital Networking: Your Virtual Rolodex

In today's digital age, online platforms have become powerful tools for expanding your professional network. LinkedIn, in particular, has emerged as the go-to hub for connecting with industry leaders, potential mentors, and like-minded professionals. Crafting a killer profile that showcases your skills and experiences is your first step towards making a memorable impression.

But don't be a wallflower – jump into the conversation. Join groups that match your interests, share your thoughts in discussions, and post content that shows off your knowledge. By being active and connecting with the big names in your field, you'll be surprised at the incredible opportunities that might come your way.

Real-World Networking: Building Connections that Count

While the digital world offers convenience, nothing quite replaces the power of face-to-face interactions. Community events, workshops, and industry conferences are where the real magic happens. You'll get to connect with like-minded people in your field, bounce ideas around, and build relationships that go beyond just a screen name.

• **Community Events:** From local meetups to industry-specific gatherings, these events offer a chance to connect with people in your area who share similar interests and career paths.

Imagine attending a local Women in Tech meetup. You might find yourself chatting with a seasoned software engineer who becomes your mentor and opens doors to her extensive network, providing invaluable guidance and opportunities.

• **Workshops and Seminars:** Attending workshops and seminars is a double win: not only do you sharpen your skills and expand your knowledge, but you also get to mingle and network with other passionate individuals.

Picture yourself in a graphic design workshop, collaborating with fellow designers on a project. This shared experience not only fosters creativity but also builds connections that could blossom into future collaborations or even job opportunities.

- **Industry Conferences:** These larger-scale events are like a networking hub for professionals. You'll find experts, leaders, and potential collaborators from all corners of your field gathered in one place.

Envision yourself attending a national tech conference where you hear a keynote speech by a renowned CEO. You muster up the courage to approach them afterward, spark a conversation, and leave such a positive impression that they invite you for an informational interview at their company.

When attending these events, be sure to come prepared with your elevator pitch, business cards, and a genuine desire to connect. Approach each interaction with curiosity and authenticity. Keep in mind: networking isn't just about collecting contacts; it's about building relationships based on mutual respect and shared interests.

By casting a wide net and embracing both online and offline networking, you'll create a strong network of professional contacts who can offer support, advice, and opportunities that can significantly boost your chances of getting that job you've always wanted.

The Follow-Up: Nurturing Connections Beyond the Initial Spark

Meeting someone at a networking event is like planting a seed. The follow-up (as I've mentioned throughout this entire book because of its huge significance) is the water and sunlight that nurture that seed into a flourishing plant. A well-crafted follow-up email or message can be the key to transforming a fleeting encounter into a lasting professional relationship.

Think of it like this: you've just met someone who could be a potential mentor, collaborator, or even employer. They've given you their time and attention, and now it's your turn to show your appreciation and continue the conversation. A thoughtful follow-up demonstrates your professionalism, initiative, and genuine interest in building a connection.

But how do you craft a follow-up that hits the right notes? Here are some tips:

- **Be Timely:** Send your follow-up email within 24-48 hours of the event. This shows you're proactive and that the conversation was meaningful to you.

- **Be Personal:** Don't just send a generic "nice to meet you" email. Personalize it by referencing something specific you discussed during your conversation.

- **Express Gratitude:** Thank the person for their time and their guidance.

- **Reiterate Your Interest:** If you're interested in a specific opportunity, reiterate your interest and highlight your relevant skills and experience.

- **Offer Value:** Share a relevant article, resource, or connection that might be helpful to the person.

Remember, the follow-up is just the beginning. Nurturing a professional relationship takes time and effort. Schedule follow-up meetings, stay in touch through email or social media, and continue to offer value and support. By investing in these relationships, you're investing in your future career success.

CRAFTING THE PERFECT RESUME

Your resume is your first impression on paper, your chance to showcase your skills, experiences, and potential to prospective employers. A well-crafted resume isn't just a formality; it's a strategic tool that can open doors to exciting career opportunities. Let's delve into crafting a standout resume that captures attention and paves the way for career advancement.

Key Elements of a Great Resume

A great resume is clear, concise, and tailored to the specific job you're applying for. It should include:

- **Compelling Summary or Objective:** A brief statement that captures your career goals and highlights your most relevant qualifications.

- **Detailed Work History:** Showcase your accomplishments and responsibilities in previous roles, using action verbs and give specific examples to show how you made a difference.

- **Skills and Qualifications:** List your most relevant skills, both hard and soft, emphasizing those that align with the job requirements.

- **Education and Certifications:** Include your educational background, relevant coursework, and any certifications you've earned.

Tailoring Your Resume for Success

One-size-fits-all resumes are a thing of the past. To stand out in today's competitive job market, you need to tailor your resume for each position you apply for. This means carefully reading through the job description, figuring out the key skills and experience the employer is looking for, and then highlighting the parts of your own experience that show you're their perfect match.

Remember, your resume is not just a list of your accomplishments; it's a story of your professional journey. By carefully curating the content and tailoring it to each opportunity, you can create a compelling narrative that showcases your value and potential to prospective employers. This will be especially valuable at career fairs where you can hand your resume directly to a recruiter who will have time to look over it.

ACING THE INTERVIEW

Congratulations on landing an interview! It's your time to shine and demonstrate why you're the ideal candidate for the job. While interviews can be nerve-wracking, remember that preparation and confidence are your allies. Let's delve into the different interview formats you might encounter and equip you with the tools to navigate them successfully.

Common Interview Formats

Interviews aren't one-size-fits-all. They come in various formats, each with its own purpose and style:

- **Traditional Interviews:** These are the standard one-on-one or panel interviews, where you'll be asked about your background, experience, skills, and overall fit for the role.

- **Behavioral Interviews:** Here, employers delve into your past experiences to predict your future performance. Expect questions that ask for specific examples of how you've handled challenges, worked in teams, or demonstrated leadership.

- **Case Interviews:** Common in consulting and finance, these interviews present you with real-world scenarios or problems to solve on the spot, assessing your analytical and problem-solving abilities.

- **Virtual Interviews:** Increasingly popular due to remote work, these interviews are conducted via video conferencing platforms like Zoom or Google Meet.

Keys to Interview Success

- **Preparation:** Preparation is the cornerstone of a successful interview. Thoroughly research the company, its mission, values, products, and recent news. This knowledge will allow you to tailor your responses to align with the company's goals and demonstrate your genuine interest in the opportunity.

- **Practice:** Practice makes perfect. Rehearse your answers to common interview questions, crafting stories that highlight your skills and experiences. Don't just memorize answers; aim for a natural, conversational tone that reflects your authentic self. Consider role-playing with a friend or family member to refine your responses and gain feedback.

- **Confidence:** Confidence is contagious. Even if you're feeling nervous, project confidence through your body language: maintain good posture, make eye contact, and offer a firm handshake. Remember to breathe deeply and focus on your strengths. Your enthusiasm and genuine interest will shine through and make a positive impression on the interviewer.

TLDR: MASTERING CAREER FAIRS, NETWORKING, AND INTERVIEWS

Here's what we covered in Chapter 8:

1. **Career Fairs: Your Networking Playground:** Career fairs offer a unique opportunity to connect with potential employers, discover hidden job openings, and practice your networking skills in a low-pressure environment.
2. **Preparation is Key:** Do your research on attending companies, craft a mind-blowing resume and elevator pitch, and dress professionally to make a strong first impression.
3. **Expand Your Network Beyond the Fair:** Explore community events, workshops, and industry conferences to connect with professionals in person. Also, leverage online platforms like LinkedIn to expand your network and showcase your professional brand.
4. **The Art of the Follow-Up:** Nurture your connections by sending personalized thank-you emails and maintaining ongoing engagement.
5. **Crafting Your Winning Resume:** Your resume is your personal marketing tool. Tailor it to each opportunity, highlighting your most relevant skills and experiences.
6. **Acing the Interview:** Understand common interview formats, practice your responses, and project confidence to showcase your best self to potential employers.

You've discovered your passions, honed your skills, and started building your network – now it's time to connect the dots and chart a course for your future.

Let's dive into the art of crafting a comprehensive career plan, a personalized roadmap that aligns with your ambitions and aspirations. Get ready to set meaningful goals, identify areas for growth, and make strategic decisions that will propel you towards the career of your dreams.

CHAPTER 9
YOUR ROADMAP TO SUCCESS

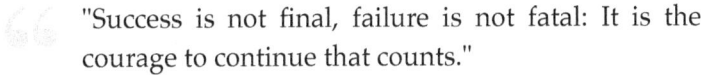

"Success is not final, failure is not fatal: It is the courage to continue that counts."

WINSTON CHURCHILL

Y ou've absorbed a lot of information throughout this book, and I wouldn't be surprised to hear that you're feeling a little overwhelmed. Sure, these pages have helped you discover a lot about yourself and the world of work, but you're probably thinking, *it's easier said than done.* So how exactly do you get the ball rolling? It starts with a simple step: turning that knowledge into a clear and achievable action plan.

Setting goals is the first part of starting your action plan–it provides the structure and support you need. In this chapter, you'll learn how to set SMART goals, break them down into achievable steps, and track your progress. By the end, you'll have a clear vision for your future, empowering you to take control and chase those dreams with confidence.

CRAFTING SMART GOALS

The SMART framework—which stands for Specific, Measurable, Achievable, Relevant, and Time-bound—is a powerful tool that helps you set goals that are not only ambitious but also realistic and attainable. This framework is especially useful when transitioning from high school and feeling overwhelmed by the many paths available.

By using SMART goals, you can transform wishy-washy dreams into crystal-clear objectives that you can practically reach out and grab. Here's how:

1. **Specific:** Instead of saying, "I want to go to college," be specific about the *type* of college and program you're interested in. Maybe your goal is to attend a four-year university with a strong environmental science program, or perhaps you're looking for a community college that offers an associate's degree in culinary arts.
2. **Measurable:** Break down your goal into smaller, measurable steps so you can see your progress and stay motivated along the way. For example, if your goal is to get accepted into a specific college, you could track your progress by completing and submitting your application, taking standardized tests like the SAT or ACT, requesting letters of recommendation, visiting the college campus for a tour or information session, and attending a college fair or virtual open house.
3. **Achievable:** While it's important to aim high, make sure your goals are realistic. Don't set yourself up for disappointment by aiming for something completely out of reach. If you're struggling in math, maybe becoming a theoretical physicist isn't the most achievable goal right now. But that doesn't mean you can't pursue a different STEM field that aligns with your strengths.

4. **Relevant:** Your goals should matter to you and fit into your bigger picture. If you're driven by social justice and advocacy, aiming for a career in law or social work could be a perfect fit. If you're fascinated by the intricate workings of the human body, perhaps a path in medicine or biomedical research would be more fulfilling.

5. **Time-bound:** Deadlines keep you on track and motivated. Set specific timelines for achieving your goals. For example, if you want to apply to college in the fall, set deadlines for completing your applications, taking standardized tests, and gathering recommendation letters.

Setting clear, specific goals will help you make informed decisions, prioritize your efforts, and stay motivated throughout your journey. Here's an example in action:

*Sophia has always dreamed of launching her own online clothing boutique. Instead of just vaguely wanting to "start a business," Sophia sets a crystal-clear goal: Launch an online clothing boutique specializing in sustainable and ethically sourced fashion. This is a **specific** and well-defined objective. To stay on track, she sets **measurable** milestones: Create a business plan by June, build an online store by August, and launch with a collection of 20 items by October. Recognizing the need to balance schoolwork with her entrepreneurial dreams, Sophia breaks down her tasks into smaller, manageable steps with **achievable** deadlines. Her passion for fashion and sustainability aligns perfectly with her business idea, making it a **relevant** and fulfilling pursuit. Finally, Sophia sets a concrete launch date for her online store: October 1st. This **time-bound** goal provides a clear target to focus her efforts.*

With her SMART goal in place, Sophia has a roadmap to follow as she starts her own business, proving that success comes from a clear vision, actionable steps, and unwavering passion.

Envision your Future

One of the most powerful things you can do to achieve your career aspirations is to paint a vivid picture of your future, just like Sophia's example. Begin by reflecting on where you envision yourself in a year. Do you see yourself excelling in your college courses, exploring different majors, or perhaps securing a summer internship?

Use all your senses to immerse yourself in that vision. Imagine the crisp smell of textbooks as you flip through pages, the sound of your professor's voice during a lecture, or the taste of coffee as you study late into the night. Feel the warmth of the sun on your skin as you stroll across campus, the excitement of meeting new classmates, or the sense of accomplishment as you ace your exams. Envision yourself in your dorm room, decorated with personal touches, or imagine your desk at your summer internship, filled with challenging projects. By tapping into your senses, you bring your vision to life and make it feel more tangible and attainable.

Next, broaden your horizon. Imagine yourself five years down the line. What professional milestones do you aspire to achieve? Are you aiming to graduate with honors? Launch your own startup? Land a fulfilling job in your chosen field? Maybe you're considering vocational school to gain hands-on skills in a trade you're passionate about. Whatever your vision, bring it to life. Feel the weight of your diploma in your hand, the thrill of pitching your business idea, or the satisfaction of completing a challenging project at your dream job. Immerse yourself in the details. What sounds and sights surround you? What emotions do you feel? The more vivid your vision, the more motivating it will be.

Once you have a clear vision, it's time to break down the journey into actionable steps. What specific actions can you take today, this week, or this month to propel yourself closer to your goals? Perhaps you need to research different colleges or vocational programs, network with alumni or professionals in your desired field, or start building your portfolio.

Remember, your career should be a reflection of your passions and skills. What activities do you genuinely enjoy? What talents do you possess that can be leveraged in a professional setting? By aligning your career with your interests, you'll find greater fulfillment and motivation along the way.

Tips to Achieve Your SMART Goals:

1. **Write it down:** Clearly define your SMART goal and the steps you'll take to get there. Display this list somewhere you'll see it regularly as a constant reminder.
2. **Set deadlines:** Establish specific dates for completing each step and track your progress.
3. **Reward yourself:** Celebrate your achievements, no matter how small, to keep yourself motivated.
4. **Find a goal partner:** Share your goals with someone who can support you and hold you accountable. Offer to reciprocate their support.

CREATING A CAREER PLAN

It's time to put everything you've learned in this book together and create a roadmap for your future. You've already mastered SMART goals for specific objectives, so now let's zoom out and craft a comprehensive plan for your career journey. Think of SMART goals as individual steps on the path toward your ultimate career destination. Your career plan, on the other hand, is the detailed map that guides you through each of those steps, ensuring you stay on course and reach your full potential.

Here's a step-by-step process to create a career plan that sets you up for success. (And remember, if you need a refresher, just flip through the chapters of this book):

1. **Self-Assessment:** Delve into your interests, strengths, values, and skills. What do you love doing? What are you naturally good at? What matters most to you? Look at your Holland Code assessment to better understand yourself; it can also help you explore career paths that align with your passions and abilities.
2. **Research:** Explore various career paths that align with your self-assessment. Read through job descriptions, career profiles, and educational requirements to get a sense of the possibilities and discover what truly excites you.
3. **Set Goals:** Craft SMART goals that align with your career aspirations. These goals should be Specific, Measurable, Achievable, Relevant, and Time-Bound. For example, instead of a vague goal like: *get a good job*, a SMART goal might be: *secure a paid internship in marketing at a tech company by the end of the summer*.
4. **Create a Plan:** Formalize your goals and the steps you'll take to achieve them in a written career plan. Include deadlines or timelines to keep yourself on track, but remember to be adaptable – your plan can evolve as you learn and grow.
5. **Take Action:** Put your career plan into motion. Gain experience through internships or volunteer work, pursue further education or training, or network with professionals in your field. Every step you take brings you closer to your ideal job.

Keep in mind that your career path is a winding road, not a straight shot to the finish line. To help you navigate the twists and turns, here are some extra tips to keep you on track:

- **Track Your Progress:** Monitor your achievements and milestones. Celebrate your successes, learn from setbacks, and adjust your plan as needed.

- **Use Your Support Network:** Don't hesitate to ask for help from your teachers, guidance counselors, family, or professionals in your desired field. Their insights and experience can be invaluable.

- **Stay Flexible:** Be open to new opportunities and be willing to adapt your plan as your interests and circumstances change.

- **Continuously Learn and Grow:** Embrace lifelong learning by expanding your knowledge and skills to stay competitive in the ever-changing job market.

- **Review and Revise:** Regularly assess your progress and make any necessary adjustments to your plan. Reflect on your journey, celebrate your achievements, and set new goals for the future.

Follow these steps, but feel free to revise your career plan as you evolve. I believe in your ability to navigate the ever-changing work world and create a career that truly reflects who you are.

INSPIRATION FOR YOUR CAREER JOURNEY

You've done the hard work of crafting your career plan – now it's time to bring it to life. Let's take inspiration from Brady, a high school senior with a passion for environmental science. Brady's story shows how taking action, breaking down goals, and using available resources can transform your aspirations into reality.

Inspired by a career planning workshop, Brady dove headfirst into researching environmental science careers. He dug deep into job descriptions, figuring out what skills he'd need to succeed. Then, he set some pretty ambitious goals for himself, like landing a summer internship at an environmental organization, volunteering for a local conservation project, and even kicking off a recycling program at his school.

But the reality of the situation quickly hit him. Landing an internship was tough, and his schedule was packed with schoolwork and extracurriculars. Rejection letters piled up, and he felt like he was barely keeping his head above water. It was overwhelming.

Remembering the advice from the workshop, Brady took a step back and broke down his goals into smaller, more manageable tasks. He created a timeline, set deadlines, and started networking like crazy. He attended environmental conferences, informational interviews, and even enrolled in an online course on sustainable agriculture. He was determined to make it work.

It wasn't easy. There were more rejections, late nights studying, and the constant worry that he wouldn't achieve his goals. But Brady kept pushing forward, seeking guidance from his biology teacher, joining environmental clubs, and finding mentors who believed in him.

And you know what? All that hard work and persistence finally paid off. Brady landed a summer internship at a local environmental nonprofit, where he gained valuable hands-on experience in conservation and advocacy. He even finished that online course and successfully launched a recycling program at his school.

Looking back, Brady knows he couldn't have done it alone. He's grateful for the support and resources he found along the way. He's learned that the path to achieving your goals isn't always easy, and there will be setbacks and unexpected challenges. But with determination, a solid plan, and a willingness to adapt, he's ready to tackle any challenge that comes his way.

Just like Brady, you have the power to turn your career plan into action. Whether you're exploring different paths, seeking internships, or developing new skills, remember these key takeaways:

- **Break down your goals:** Tackle them one step at a time.

- **Stay resilient:** Challenges are inevitable, but don't give up.

- **Utilize resources:** Seek guidance from teachers, mentors, and family.

With determination, perseverance, and the right tools, you'll be well on your way to crafting the fulfilling career you've been dreaming of.

RESOURCES TO GUIDE YOU

Need a little guidance as you embark on your career journey? The following websites and organizations offer a range of resources to help you explore different career paths, make informed decisions, and access support for your professional development.

Websites

Career Exploration for Teens: This website is packed with resources to help you explore different career paths, including self-assessments, career profiles, and information on education and training options.

https://content.ces.ncsu.edu/career-exploration-for-teens

Kids Money: If you need information on managing finances, exploring career options, or preparing for college, this hub is a great place to start.

https://www.kidsmoney.org/teens/careers/high-school-resources/

Learning Liftoff: This platform offers high school students a variety of career planning resources, including information on STEM careers, college planning, and scholarships.

https://learningliftoff.com/career/stem-careers/5-essential-career-planning-resources-for-high-school-students/

Organizations

Career One Stop: Sponsored by the U.S. Department of Labor, this website offers comprehensive career resources, including job search tools, career exploration guides, and information on training and education programs. https://www.careeronestop.org/

National Career Development Association (NCDA): This professional organization provides resources and support for career counselors and individuals seeking career guidance. https://www.ncda.org/

TLDR: CHARTING YOUR COURSE

Chapter 9 focused on bringing together everything you've learned throughout the book. We explored how to envision your future, set goals, and create a strong plan to make that vision a reality. Here's what we covered:

- **SMART Goals:** Turn dreams into clear, achievable steps. Be specific, measurable, realistic, relevant, and time-bound.

- **Envision Your Future:** Imagine yourself in one and five years to stay motivated. Use all your senses to paint a vivid picture of where you want to be, what you'll be doing, and how you'll feel.

- **Career Planning:** Formalize your goals and the steps you'll take to achieve them in a written career plan. This plan should include your education goals, networking strategies, and timeline for achieving your objectives.

Whew, we've covered a ton in this book! From figuring out what makes you tick to navigating the intense world of job hunting and interviews, you've learned a lot about taking charge of your future. We've talked about how the expectations from family, school, and society can sometimes feel like a heavy weight, but you have the power to break free and chase your own dreams. Remember, it's all about discovering what lights your fire, challenging those old stereotypes, and surrounding yourself with people who believe in you.

We've explored many different career paths, from science and tech to business and the arts, and even the exciting world of entrepreneurship. You've also got a whole toolbox of strategies for acing those career fairs, networking like a pro, and rocking those interviews.

But now comes the truly empowering part: taking all this valuable knowledge and turning it into action. In the conclusion of this book, we'll explore how to put your newfound knowledge into action, overcome any remaining obstacles, and create a clear path towards the future you want.

So get ready, because your success story is just getting started!

CONCLUSION

Throughout this book, we've explored the exciting, sometimes daunting, world of career planning. We've discovered that your career isn't just a job; it's a journey of self-discovery, growth, and impact. It's about finding what inspires you, and pursuing it with passion and determination.

Remember Mayra, torn between her love for science and her passion for art? She brilliantly merged her passions, pursuing a degree in scientific illustration. Now, she uses her artistic talents to bring complex scientific concepts to life, creating beautiful and informative visuals that can be found in textbooks, scientific journals, and museum exhibits. Five years later, Mayra is thriving as a scientific illustrator, a testament to her dedication and the power of taking control of one's future.

You now have the tools and knowledge to do the same. You know how to identify your strengths, explore career paths, set SMART goals, and build a support network. You're prepared to ace interviews, network like a pro, and even launch your own business if that's your dream.

But the real magic happens when you take action. Don't let this book gather dust on a shelf. Use it as your guide, your roadmap to success. Update your plans as you grow, and don't be afraid to seize new opportunities as they arise.

Your future self will thank you for the effort you put in today. So, take that first step. Start exploring, start learning, start building the career you deserve.

Remember, the journey of a thousand miles begins with a single step. Take that step today. Your success story starts now.

REFERENCES

ALIS Alberta. (n.d.). How to discuss career plans with your family. Retrieved from https://alis.alberta.ca/plan-your-career/how-to-discuss-career-plans-with-your-family/

ALIS Alberta. (n.d.). Take action to achieve your career goals. Retrieved from https://alis.alberta.ca/plan-your-career/take-action-to-achieve-your-career-goals/

ALIS Alberta. (n.d.). Your passion can inspire your future career. Retrieved from https://alis.alberta.ca/plan-your-career/learn-more-about-yourself/your-passion-can-inspire-your-future-career/

Aspiring Youths. (n.d.). Advantages and disadvantages of adult education. Retrieved from https://aspiringyouths.com/advantages-disadvantages/adult-education-2/

Barclays LifeSkills. (n.d.). 5 ways to find out what you're good at. Retrieved from https://barclayslifeskills.com/i-want-to-choose-my-next-step/school/5-ways-to-find-out-what-you-re-good-at/

BetterUp. (n.d.). Networking. Retrieved from https://www.betterup.com/blog/networking

BetterUp. (n.d.). What is career coaching. Retrieved from https://www.betterup.com/blog/what-is-career-coaching

Best Colleges. (n.d.). Affordable online schools. Retrieved from https://www.bestcolleges.com/online-schools/affordable/

Best Colleges. (n.d.). Careers in art and design. Retrieved from https://www.bestcolleges.com/careers/art-and-design/

Best Colleges. (n.d.). Careers in STEM. Retrieved from https://www.bestcolleges.com/careers/stem/

Best Colleges. (n.d.). Choosing a major. Retrieved from https://www.bestcolleges.com/resources/choosing-a-major/

Best Colleges. (n.d.). How to choose the right college. Retrieved from https://www.bestcolleges.com/blog/how-to-choose-the-right-college/

Best Colleges. (n.d.). Pros and cons of trade school. Retrieved from https://www.bestcolleges.com/resources/career-training/pros-and-cons-trade-school/

Blinkist. (n.d.). Essential online networking tips. Retrieved from https://www.blinkist.com/magazine/posts/essential-online-networking-tips

Boston University. (2021). Career assessment tests. Retrieved from https://www.bu.edu/pdpa/files/2021/04/Career-Assessment-Tests.pdf

British Style Society. (n.d.). Pros and cons of life in the creative industries.

REFERENCES

Retrieved from https://britishstylesociety.uk/pros-and-cons-to-life-in-the-creative-industries

Bureau of Labor Statistics. (2015). Career planning for high schoolers. Retrieved from https://www.bls.gov/careeroutlook/2015/article/career-planning-for-high-schoolers.htm

Calling All Optimists. (n.d.). Why career planning is important for success. Retrieved from https://callingalloptimists.com/why-career-planning-is-important-for-success/

Capital One. (n.d.). Alternatives to college. Retrieved from https://www.capitalone.com/learn-grow/life-events/alternatives-to-college/

Career Addict. (n.d.). Teen entrepreneurs. Retrieved from https://www.careeraddict.com/teen-entrepreneurs

Career Explorer Hawaii. (n.d.). Career clusters. Retrieved from https://careerexplorer.hawaii.edu/assessments/career_clusters.php

Career Fair Plus. (n.d.). Benefits of attending college career fairs. Retrieved from https://www.careerfairplus.com/blog/benefits-of-attending-college-career-fairs

Career Fair Plus. (n.d.). Prepare for a career fair. Retrieved from https://www.careerfairplus.com/blog/prepare-for-a-career-fair

Career Fair Plus. (n.d.). Reasons to attend a career fair. Retrieved from https://www.careerfairplus.com/blog/6-reasons-why-you-need-to-attend-a-career-fair

Career Key. (n.d.). Career clusters and career pathways. Retrieved from https://www.careerkey.org/fit/clusters-pathways/career-clusters-and-career-pathways

Career Key. (n.d.). Career clusters map. Retrieved from https://static1.squarespace.com/static/5ea9b3d-c4a1d870f88a99f57/t/61cf9f64c369225600e84645/1640996708592/Career_Key_career-clusters-map.pdf

Career Masterclass. (n.d.). 6 benefits of career planning. Retrieved from https://careermasterclass.com/6-benefits-of-career-planning-2/

Career Profiles. (n.d.). Business careers. Retrieved from https://www.careerprofiles.info/business-careers.html

Career Tech. (n.d.). Career clusters. Retrieved from https://careertech.org/career-clusters

Career Tech. (n.d.). Career clusters student interest survey. Retrieved from https://careertech.org/resource/career-clusters-student-interest-survey

CareerWise. (n.d.). Cluster pathway. Retrieved from https://careerwise.minnstate.edu/careers/cluster-pathway.html

CareerWise. (n.d.). Job fairs. Retrieved from https://careerwise.minnstate.edu/jobs/job-fairs.html

CareerWise. (n.d.). What is a career cluster? Retrieved from https://careerwise.minnstate.edu/mymncareers/finish-school/what-is-a-career-cluster.html

REFERENCES

Careers at University of Maryland, Baltimore County. (n.d.). Self-assessment. Retrieved from https://careers.umbc.edu/students/discover/self/assess-ds/

Careers at University of Utah. (n.d.). Peaks and valleys. Retrieved from https://careers.utah.edu/peaks-and-valleys/29/

Chron. (n.d.). Benefits of early career exploration. Retrieved from https://work.chron.com/benefits-early-career-exploration-2174.html

Chron. (n.d.). Career interest surveys for teenagers. Retrieved from https://work.chron.com/career-interest-surveys-teenagers-17437.html

Chron. (n.d.). Family factors influencing career choices. Retrieved from https://work.chron.com/family-factors-influencing-career-choices-11176.html

Chron. (n.d.). How to prepare for a job fair. Retrieved from https://www.indeed.com/career-advice/finding-a-job/how-to-prepare-for-a-job-fair

Chron. (n.d.). The role of career planning and district success. Retrieved from https://kuder.com/blog/the-role-of-career-planning-and-district-success/

Classplus. (n.d.). Ways teachers help students with career options. Retrieved from https://classplusapp.com/growth/5-ways-teachers-help-students-with-career-options/

College Raptor. (n.d.). Pros and cons: Job college. Retrieved from https://www.collegeraptor.com/find-colleges/articles/student-life/pros-cons-job-college/

College Reality Check. (n.d.). Employers care about college rankings. Retrieved from https://collegerealitycheck.com/employers-care-about-college-rankings/

Colleges of Distinction. (n.d.). Top 50 questions to ask your guidance counselor. Retrieved from https://collegesofdistinction.com/advice/top-50-questions-to-ask-your-guidance-counselor/

Concordia University of Edmonton. (n.d.). Career fair resources. Retrieved from https://concordia.ab.ca/student-services/career-services/career-resources/career-development-resources/why-attend-a-career-fair-even-when-you-dont-think-you-need-to/

CreativeLive. (n.d.). 25 creative jobs career paths for creative people. Retrieved from https://www.creativelive.com/blog/25-creative-jobs-career-paths-for-creative-people/

eLearning Industry. (n.d.). Advantages and disadvantages of online learning. Retrieved from https://elearningindustry.com/advantages-and-disadvan-tages-online-learning

Education Compass. (n.d.). Top 5 reasons to choose a vocational education. Retrieved from https://www.educationcompass.com/advice-central/top-5-reasons-to-choose-a-vocational-education/

Education Corner. (n.d.). Benefits of earning a college degree. Retrieved from https://www.educationcorner.com/benefit-of-earning-a-college-degree.html

ERIC. (2021). Successful people college. Retrieved from https://files.eric.ed.gov/fulltext/ED613575.pdf

REFERENCES

Federal Trade Commission. (n.d.). Choosing a vocational school or certificate program. Retrieved from https://consumer.ftc.gov/articles/choosing-vocational-school-or-certificate-program

Forbes. (2021). How to set career goals and achieve them. Retrieved from https://www.forbes.com/sites/carolinecastrillon/2021/12/26/how-to-set-career-goals-and-achieve-them/?sh=59c169271aa1

Forbes. (2021). Not your parents' career. Retrieved from https://www.forbes.com/sites/markcperna/2021/11/16/not-your-parents-career-or-is-it-parents-exert-significant-influence-on-kids-career-choices/?sh=2845d085c1c9

Forbes. (2022). What does a career coach do? Eight ways they may be able to help. Retrieved from https://www.forbes.com/sites/forbescoachescouncil/2022/07/14/what-does-a-career-coach-do-eight-ways-they-may-be-able-to-help/?sh=33959535506f

Franklin University. (n.d.). Choose your career before choosing your college degree. Retrieved from https://www.franklin.edu/blog/choose-your-career-before-choosing-your-college-degree

FreshBooks. (n.d.). How do I get money to start my business? Retrieved from https://www.freshbooks.com/hub/startup/how-do-i-get-money-to-start-my-business

Get Into Energy. (n.d.). STEM skills list. Retrieved from https://stem.getintoenergy.com/stem-skills-list/

Global Career Counsellor. (n.d.). How can a teacher help in student career guidance. Retrieved from https://www.globalcareercounsellor.com/blog/how-can-a-teacher-help-in-student-career-guidance/

Global Citizen Year. (n.d.). Alternatives to college. Retrieved from https://www.globalcitizenyear.org/content/alternatives-to-college/

Great Business Schools. (n.d.). How to network online. Retrieved from https://www.greatbusinessschools.org/how-to-network-online/

Gwynedd Mercy University. (n.d.). Careers in finance. Retrieved from https://www.gmercyu.edu/academics/learn/careers-in-finance

Handshake. (n.d.). Finance internships. Retrieved from https://joinhandshake.com/blog/students/finance-internships/

Harvard Business Review. (1985). How to write a winning business plan. Retrieved from https://hbr.org/1985/05/how-to-write-a-winning-business-plan

Harvard Business School Online. (n.d.). Career advancement. Retrieved from https://online.hbs.edu/blog/post/career-advancement

Harvard Business School Online. (n.d.). Entrepreneurial skills. Retrieved from https://online.hbs.edu/blog/post/entrepreneurial-skills

Harvard Business School Online. (n.d.). Finance skills employers look for on a resume. Retrieved from https://online.hbs.edu/blog/post/finance-skills-employers-look-for-on-a-resume

Headspace. (n.d.). Career plan template. Retrieved from https://headspace.org.au/explore-topics/for-young-people/career-plan-template/

REFERENCES

Herriman Telegraph. (n.d.). Pros and cons of going to college. Retrieved from https://herrimantelegraph.org/1967/oped/pros-and-cons-of-going-to-college/

High5Test. (n.d.). Identifying personal strengths. Retrieved from https://high-5test.com/identifying-personal-strengths/

Hays. (n.d.). Career advice: Career development. Retrieved from https://www.hays.com.au/career-advice/career-development/setting-career-goals

Human Capital Online. (n.d.). Significance of societal perception and self-identity in making career choices. Retrieved from https://www.humancapitalonline.-com/Significance-of-Societal-Perception-and-Self-Identity-in-Making-Career-Choices

Indeed. (n.d.). Advantages of entrepreneurship. Retrieved from https://www.indeed.com/career-advice/finding-a-job/advantages-entrepreneurship

Indeed. (n.d.). Business careers. Retrieved from https://www.indeed.com/career-advice/finding-a-job/business-careers

Indeed. (n.d.). Business jobs entry level. Retrieved from https://www.indeed.-com/career-advice/finding-a-job/business-jobs-entry-level

Indeed. (n.d.). Career counseling questions to ask. Retrieved from https://www.indeed.com/career-advice/career-development/career-coun-selling-questions-to-ask

Indeed. (n.d.). Career goal setting. Retrieved from https://www.indeed.com/career-advice/career-development/career-goal-setting

Indeed. (n.d.). College careers. Retrieved from https://www.indeed.com/career-advice/finding-a-job/college-careers

Indeed. (n.d.). Entrepreneurial skills. Retrieved from https://www.indeed.-com/career-advice/career-development/entrepreneurial-skills

Indeed. (n.d.). Family factors influencing career choices. Retrieved from https://work.chron.com/family-factors-influencing-career-choices-11176.html

Indeed. (n.d.). Finance career job outlook. Retrieved from https://www.indeed.-com/career-advice/finding-a-job/finance-career-job-outlook

Indeed. (n.d.). How to craft a professional resume. Retrieved from https://www.indeed.com/career-advice/resumes-cover-letters/how-to-craft-a-professional-resume

Indeed. (n.d.). How to find your passion. Retrieved from https://www.indeed.-com/career-advice/finding-a-job/how-to-find-your-passion

Indeed. (n.d.). How to prepare for a job fair. Retrieved from https://www.in-deed.com/career-advice/finding-a-job/how-to-prepare-for-a-job-fair

Indeed. (n.d.). Jobs that require college degrees. Retrieved from https://www.in-deed.com/career-advice/finding-a-job/jobs-that-require-college-degrees

Indeed. (n.d.). Make a career plan. Retrieved from https://www.indeed.com/career-advice/career-development/make-a-career-plan

REFERENCES

Indeed. (n.d.). Networking follow-up email. Retrieved from https://www.indeed.com/career-advice/career-development/networking-follow-up-email

Indiana STEM Network. (n.d.). STEM career opportunities. Retrieved from https://www.istemnetwork.org/parents-students/stem-career-opportunities/

Institute of Entrepreneurship Development. (n.d.). Cultural skills for today's youth. Retrieved from https://ied.eu/blog/culture-blog/from-passion-to-profession-the-must-have-cultural-skills-for-todays-youth/

InterCoast Colleges. (n.d.). How to choose a trade school that suits your needs. Retrieved from https://intercoast.edu/blog/how-to-choose-a-trade-school-that-suits-your-needs/

Job Test. (n.d.). Career test for teens. Retrieved from https://www.jobtest.org/career-test/for-teens

Kuder. (n.d.). The role of career planning and district success. Retrieved from https://kuder.com/blog/the-role-of-career-planning-and-district-success/

Learn How to Become. (n.d.). Finance business careers. Retrieved from https://www.learnhowtobecome.org/finance-business-careers/

Learning Lift Off. (n.d.). Career planning resources for high school students. Retrieved from https://learningliftoff.com/career/stem-careers/5-essential-career-planning-resources-for-high-school-students/

Lifology Magazine. (n.d.). Career anxieties among teenagers. Lifology. Retrieved from https://magazine.lifology.com/career/career-anxieties-among-teenagers/

LinkedIn. (n.d.). Best places to network. Retrieved from https://www.indeed.com/career-advice/career-development/best-places-to-network

LinkedIn. (n.d.). Best way to approach potential mentor career. Retrieved from https://www.linkedin.com/advice/3/what-best-way-approach-potential-mentor-career

LinkedIn. (n.d.). Career choices: Importance of aligning your passion. Retrieved from https://www.linkedin.com/pulse/career-choices-importance-aligning-your-passion-murtaza-khurshid

LinkedIn. (n.d.). Crafting the perfect resume: Essential tips. Retrieved from https://www.linkedin.com/pulse/crafting-perfect-resume-cv-essential-tips-success-cvexamples

LinkedIn. (n.d.). Why should career plans be aligned with interests and abilities. Retrieved from https://www.linkedin.com/pulse/why-should-career-plans-aligned-interests-abilities-naarayan-c-l-

MensLine Australia. (n.d.). The power of a good support network. Retrieved from https://mensline.org.au/mens-mental-health/the-power-of-a-good-support-network/

Michael Page. (n.d.). Benefits of networking. Retrieved from https://www.michaelpage.com.au/advice/career-advice/career-progression/top-12-benefits-networking-why-networking-important

National University. (n.d.). Weighing the pros and cons of online vs. in-person learning. Retrieved from https://www.nu.edu/blog/weighing-the-pros-and-cons-of-online-vs-in-person-learning/

NerdWallet. (n.d.). Business plan. Retrieved from https://www.nerdwallet.com/article/small-business/business-plan

North Carolina State University. (n.d.). Career exploration for teens. Retrieved from https://content.ces.ncsu.edu/career-exploration-for-teens

OECD Forum. (n.d.). Young people don't feel ready for the future of work. OECD. Retrieved from https://www.oecd-forum.org/posts/53006-young-people-dont-feel-ready-for-the-future-of-work

Online Manipal. (n.d.). Choosing the right online course for career development. Retrieved from https://www.onlinemanipal.com/blogs/how-to-choose-the-right-online-course-for-career-development

OpenGrowth. (n.d.). How do internal factors influence your career path. Retrieved from https://www.shellye.opengrowth.com/article/how-do-internal-factors-influence-your-career-path

Our Lady of the Lake University. (n.d.). Counselors help students career. Retrieved from https://onlineprograms.ollusa.edu/resources/article/counselors-help-students-career/

Peace University. (n.d.). Why is higher education important? Retrieved from https://www.peace.edu/news/why-is-higher-education-important/

PDPFyns. (n.d.). Finding your strengths. Retrieved from https://pdpfyns.com/finding-your-strengths/

Prep Expert. (n.d.). Pros and cons of STEM education. Retrieved from https://prepexpert.com/stem-pros-and-cons/

Prepory. (n.d.). Career clusters. Retrieved from https://prepory.com/blog/career-clusters/

Rochester City School District. (n.d.). Career interest survey. Retrieved from https://www.rcsdk12.org/cms/lib/NY01001156/Centricity/Domain/4459/Career%20Interest%20Survey.pdf

Robert Half. (n.d.). Career advice: Interview. Retrieved from https://www.roberthalf.com.au/career-advice/interview

Robert Half. (n.d.). Your career in finance. Retrieved from https://www.roberthalf.com/us/en/insights/career-development/your-career-in-finance-10-skills-that-really-count

Shorelight. (n.d.). Career action plan in 4 steps. Retrieved from https://shorelight.com/student-stories/career-action-plan-in-4-steps/

Small Business Administration. (n.d.). Steps to start your business. Retrieved from https://www.sba.gov/business-guide/10-steps-start-your-business

SoFi. (n.d.). Pros and cons of college. Retrieved from https://www.sofi.com/learn/content/pros-and-cons-of-college/

South Bay Workforce Investment Board. (n.d.). Youth success stories. Retrieved from https://www.sbwib.org/youth-success-stories

South Australia Government. (n.d.). STEM learning career pathways. Retrieved

REFERENCES

from https://www.education.sa.gov.au/parents-and-families/curriculum-and-learning/stem-learning/stem-career-pathways

StratoStar. (n.d.). Advantages of STEM careers. Retrieved from https://stratostar.com/advantages-of-stem-careers/

Student Caffe. (n.d.). Choosing a vocational program. Retrieved from http://studentcaffe.com/apply/vocational-education/choosing-a-program

Sun Myke. (n.d.). Advantages and disadvantages of adult education. Retrieved from https://sunmyke.com/blog/advantages-and-disadvantages-of-adult-education

Taylor's University. (n.d.). College life helps to develop personal growth. Retrieved from https://college.taylors.edu.my/en/life-at-taylors/news-events/news/4-ways-college-life-helps-to-develop-your-personal-growth.html

Teachmint. (n.d.). How can teachers help students with career options. Retrieved from https://blog.teachmint.com/how-can-teachers-help-students-with-career-options/

Teal HQ. (n.d.). How to find your career passion. Retrieved from https://www.tealhq.com/post/how-to-find-your-career-passion

The Muse. (n.d.). 6 fresh ways to find your passion. Retrieved from https://www.themuse.com/advice/6-fresh-ways-to-find-your-passion

The Muse. (n.d.). How to make a resume: Examples. Retrieved from https://www.themuse.com/advice/how-to-make-a-resume-examples

The Muse. (n.d.). The ultimate interview guide. Retrieved from https://www.themuse.com/advice/the-ultimate-interview-guide-30-prep-tips-for-job-interview-success

Times News Group. (n.d.). Tips on choosing adult education courses to study. Retrieved from https://timesnewsgroup.com.au/surfcoasttimes/news/tips-on-choosing-adult-education-courses-to-study/

Times of India. (n.d.). Discuss career plans with your family. Retrieved from https://toistudent.timesofindia.indiatimes.com/news/how-to/discuss-career-plans-with-your-family/80979.html

Udacity. (2022). How to build a freelance portfolio. Retrieved from https://www.udacity.com/blog/2022/06/how-to-build-a-freelance-portfolio.html

University of Florida. (n.d.). How to talk about career goals with your family during the holidays. Retrieved from https://career.ufl.edu/how-to-talk-about-career-goals-with-your-family-during-the-holidays/

University of Kansas Edwards Campus. (n.d.). 10 tips for choosing a major. Retrieved from https://edwardscampus.ku.edu/blog/10-tips-choosing-major

University of Massachusetts Global. (n.d.). Pros and cons: Working or going back to college. Retrieved from https://www.umassglobal.edu/news-and-events/blog/pros-and-cons-working-or-going-back-to-college

University of People. (n.d.). Benefits of education are societal and personal.

REFERENCES

Retrieved from https://www.uopeople.edu/blog/benefits-of-education-are-societal-and-personal/

University of South Florida Admissions. (n.d.). Top considerations when choosing a college major. Retrieved from https://admissions.usf.edu/blog/top-considerations-when-choosing-a-college-major

UCanGo2. (n.d.). Career interest survey. Retrieved from https://www.ucango2.org/publications/student/Career_Interest_Survey.pdf

Verywell Mind. (n.d.). Social support for psychological health. Retrieved from https://www.verywellmind.com/social-support-for-psychological-health-4119970

William Peace University. (n.d.). Why is higher education important? Retrieved from https://www.peace.edu/news/why-is-higher-education-important/

Work It Daily. (n.d.). How to prepare for a job fair. Retrieved from https://www.workitdaily.com/how-to-prepare-job-fair

Youth Central. (n.d.). How to create a career plan. Retrieved from https://www.youthcentral.vic.gov.au/jobs-and-careers/plan-your-career/how-to-create-a-career-plan

Youth Inc. Magazine. (n.d.). Easy ways of discussing your career plans with your parents. Retrieved from https://youthincmag.com/4-easy-ways-of-discussing-your-career-plans-with-your-parents

YouTube. (n.d.). Career advancement. Retrieved from https://www.youtube.com/watch?v=TD8VG40HJII

Zippia. (n.d.). Research skills. Retrieved from https://www.zippia.com/advice/research-skills/